Fic
Mik

Paul B. Wagner
Learning Center

4/01

North Syracuse Sr. High School

1. All pupils in the school are entitled to use the learning center and to draw materials.
2. Materials may be retained for two weeks.
3. Injury to materials beyond reasonable wear and all losses shall be paid for.
4. No materials may be taken from the learning center without being charged.

PAST FORGIVING

PAST FORGIVING

Gloria D. Miklowitz

SIMON & SCHUSTER
BOOKS FOR YOUNG READERS

SIMON & SCHUSTER BOOKS FOR YOUNG READERS
An imprint of Simon & Schuster Children's Publishing Division
1230 Avenue of the Americas, New York, New York 10020
Copyright © 1995 by Gloria D. Miklowitz
SIMON & SCHUSTER BOOKS FOR YOUNG READERS
is a trademark of Simon & Schuster.
Book design by Paul Zakris
The text for this book is set in 12-point Sabon
Manufactured in the United States of America
10   9   8   7   6

Library of Congress Cataloging-in-Publication Data

Miklowitz, Gloria D.
Past Forgiving / Gloria Miklowitz.
p. cm.
Summary: Fifteen-year-old Alexandra finds that her
boyfriend Cliff demands all her time, isolates her by his
jealousy, and finally becomes physically abusive.
[1. Aquaintance rape—Fiction. 2. Rape—Fiction
3. Dating violence—Fiction.] I. Title
PZ7.M593Pas 1995   [Fic]—dc20   94-13057

ISBN 0-671-88442-5

To David Gale,
whose thoughtful editing
made this a better book

ONE

Alexandra closed her eyes and tightly clasped her cold, damp hands. *Oh, please,* she prayed silently. *Oh, please let me get the job!*

Cliff had driven her to the Y and was waiting for her outside, in the Y parking lot. "Play it cool," he'd advised. "Don't get all gushy like you do sometimes. The reason Wilson didn't choose you the first time around was probably because you get so excited you're like a little kid. If you want her to forget you're fifteen, don't gush!"

"Gush? Do I gush?" she'd asked.

"Uh-huh!" He grinned. "Which is exactly what *I* love about you!"

"Okay. I won't gush."

"And don't go on and on about storytelling."

"But it might be useful! I mean..."

Cliff rolled his eyes and shook his head.

"Okay. I won't go on and on about storytelling."

"And wear that shirt I like—the one with the 'Save the Rain Forest' logo."

"Okay, I'll wear that shirt."

"Good, Cone. Now come here and let me give you a good-luck kiss."

Her name was Alexandra, though most people called her Alex. Cliff had called her "Cone" from the first day they'd met at the amusement park. She'd bumped into him with a drippy ice-cream cone in hand. "Hey, *watch* it!" His angry tone scared her but when he saw her fear he introduced himself and turned gentle. Ever since, whenever he was feeling especially affectionate, he called her Cone.

Now, as she waited for the interview with Ms. Wilson, she tried to remember all Cliff's advice. What to say, what not to say. To keep eye contact, how to sit, and much more. If it hadn't been for the counselor who dropped out she wouldn't even have this second interview, this second chance. "Just think," Cliff had said when they both applied a month ago. "It's perfect. If we both get Y jobs we'll be together all summer. I could pick you up each day and drive you home and we'd be taking the kids to the beach and on picnics and to Disneyland! What a blast!"

The possibility had made her dizzy—to be near Cliff every day, every hour of the summer! She knew, too, that if *she* didn't get the job some other girl would. Maybe Cliff would drive *her* to the Y and home. Think what could happen!

They had hired Cliff, not her. All month she worried. Maybe Cliff might find someone he liked better. What he saw in her was a marvel, anyway. She was too young to interest a senior and no beauty like Karen, his last girlfriend. Her nose was a bit too big and her hair hung as limp as wet noodles. Still, he called her beautiful and said looks didn't matter, anyway. Her personality and spirit mattered.

No one had ever said anything so special about her before.

She knew why *she* wanted *him*. Because he knew so much about everything, and everyone at school seemed to admire him, so that being his girl made her a kind of celebrity. And because for all his seeming self-assurance, down deep he was really vulnerable and only she knew it. He needed her, he said, because she loved him unconditionally, which no one ever had.

"Alexandra?" the woman at the Y reception desk asked at last. "Ms. Wilson will see you now. Down that hall. Third door to the right."

Alexandra jumped to her feet, wiped damp palms on her new jeans, and flew down the hall. The squeal of sneakers and grunts of effort seeped from under double doors where kids were playing basketball. Two women in sweats ambled out of the locker room carrying wet bathing suits and smelling of chlorine. A small girl in a tutu ran by.

Ms. Wilson was a large, motherly-looking woman.

She sat behind a desk in a cubbyhole room full of cluttered shelves.

"Alexandra. Nice to see you again." Ms. Wilson half raised herself and reached across her desk to shake Alex's hand, then dropped back in her seat and opened a file. "I called you because it turns out we have another summer counselor position to fill after all. One of our new hires canceled just yesterday and camp starts next week. I take it you're still interested?"

"Oh, yes!"

"Good." Ms. Wilson smiled. "I didn't offer you the job before because, frankly, I thought you were a bit young. Most of our counselors are seventeen and older."

"I see."

"So tell me why I should choose you over the others I'm considering." Ms. Wilson leaned forward and clasped her hands.

Alex took a deep breath and sat straighter. Cliff had coached her. She should speak up, look Ms. Wilson straight in the eye, and elaborate on what was already in her application. "And, whatever you do, leave out the *er*s and *uh*s," he had said.

"Take your time," Ms. Wilson prompted.

Perspiration dripped down Alex's neck and back. It was all in that file folder in front of Ms. Wilson, so why did she have to ask? Her *age*. That was the weakness. She had to persuade the woman that despite her age she could control little kids.

"I've been babysitting since I was ten," Alex said. "Friday and Saturday nights, and last summer—all day, five days a week, for one family. I have a nine-year-old sister so I have experience with that age group. I tutored some second-graders in reading."

"Yes, that's in your application. Anything else?"

"Uh, er..." Alex looked away. Should she talk about the storytelling? Would it help her be a better counselor with that background? But Cliff had said... "I like to tell stories!" she blurted. "Not just *read* stories to children, but *tell* them. You know? Without a book? Like it was happening to *me*?" She felt the excitement rising as she explained how she'd taken storytelling for fun in junior high and learned how to choose a tale that meant something special to her, then embellish it and tell it in her own words. She raced on, trying to say everything that came into her head.

"So you see," she said at last, "it's magical. I forget who I am sometimes and become my character, even wearing the clothes she might wear." She took a quick breath and rushed on. "When it's going right, I can just *feel* it!" She stopped suddenly, aware of the expression on Ms. Wilson's face. Oh, dear! She'd done it again—gushed!

Ms. Wilson smiled like she was amused. "Do you think you could teach that to children?"

"Oh, yes!"

"Super." Wilson scribbled something on Alex's file.

"Thank you, Alexandra. We'll let you know. As I said, we're considering other applicants." She stood and offered a hand again. "If we can't use you, I hope you'll apply again next year. I think you'd make a fine counselor. Good luck, dear."

Good luck! That meant *good-bye!* The words rang in Alex's ears as she retraced her steps down the hall to the reception area and out the door. Good-bye to all her dreams of what the summer could be. Good-bye to meeting other teenage counselors. To outings in the mountains and the ocean with the children. To being near Cliff.

Instead, she'd have to take the job sitting with the Taylor kids. Although she liked them and had looked forward to it, she'd be confined in the same house all summer with three little kids, trying to keep them amused and happy.

She raced down the stairs to the parking lot, looking for Cliff. Cliff had said the call back probably meant the job was hers, not that she had to compete again with older applicants. She needed his reassuring hug. She needed him to say, "It's okay. We'll still have evenings and weekends together." But when she saw him below, leaning against his red Mustang, he wasn't alone.

"Hi, guys!" Alex greeted, her eyes flitting from Cliff's animated face to the girl beside him—Karen. What was *she* doing here?

"Hey, Cone! How'd it go?" Cliff held out a hand and pulled her to him.

"Cone? He calls you Cone?" Karen said. "Conehead? What's it mean?"

Cliff grinned and hugged her tighter. "Our secret."

Alex gazed up at him, resisting the urge to brush the lock of hair from his eye.

"Guess what?" Cliff asked. "Karen's gonna be a counselor here, too!"

"Great!" Alex said with enthusiasm she didn't feel.

"So, what did Wilson say? You in, or what?"

"She'll let me know."

"It's not set? Did you say what I told you? You didn't go on and on about that storytelling stuff, I hope!"

"No! No!" she said quickly, glancing at Karen. "There's still a chance, Cliff. I think she liked me...." She heard the unpleasant whine in her voice that Cliff always hated.

"This is where I bow out," Karen said. "Don't fight, guys." She sauntered off with a backward wave of a hand. "Play nice!"

Cliff glared at Karen's back. "That girl really knows how to get under my skin!"

"Huh? What did she say?"

"Nothing! Look, Cone. It's okay. If you get the job it will be great. If you don't we'll still get together plenty this summer, so don't worry." He held out his arms and she melted right into them. "It's just that I hate having you out of my sight for even a minute."

"Me too," she mumbled into his chest, the fear subsiding. She loved the smell of him, the solid feel of his body, the safety she felt in his arms. Lately she became almost physically ill at the slightest critical look or word. What if he was tiring of her?

"Cliff?" she asked, softly, as he drove her home. "Please don't think I'm silly, but I have to ask something."

He took his right hand from the steering wheel and covered her knee. "Sure, Cone. Ask away."

She squirmed slightly, embarrassed at having to put words to her anxiety, but if she didn't know she'd be tormented all summer with doubt. And if he lied, she'd know. She could read his every small gesture, his every slight change of tone.

"I think Karen still likes you."

"Oh, come on!" Cliff looked pleased and surprised.

"I'm not kidding. Maybe you don't see it, but I do. Why did you break up?" If she could know, then maybe she could prevent the same thing happening to her. She stared straight ahead as the familiar houses and streets passed before her eyes.

"Come on! I've told you before. It's not worth talking about!"

"Tell me again. She's so pretty and nice, and she's a good artist and can talk sports like a guy. And, you *used* to like her—so what happened?"

"We just stopped getting along."

"Why? Were you bored? What do you mean?"

"Alexandra!"

"Don't make fun of me. If you're going to be working near her all summer, I have to know."

"All right. The truth?"

She swung around so she could watch his eyes.

He smiled at the road. "The truth is... I just... got tired of her bossiness." His smile vanished. "She doesn't let a guy just be a guy."

"Meaning?"

"I couldn't relax around her. She challenged everything I said. I just... well... she really knew how to get under my skin!"

Alex smiled to herself. "I'm not like that?"

He glanced her way. "You're *not* like that. I can tell you anything and you'll still like me. You're all female. Satisfied?"

She put her hand over his on the steering wheel. "Satisfied."

"Besides," he added, flashing a wicked grin. "She didn't turn me on like you do!"

She giggled and moved closer. Cliff pulled into her driveway and cut the engine, then tilted his head in the endearing way that always made her turn soft. "Are you happy now? Did I answer your question right?" He took her hands.

"Yes, but please don't get angry with me like you did back in the parking lot. Please. It scares me."

"I wasn't angry with *you*, Cone; I was angry with *me*. I hate the thought of you being away from me all summer where I can't know what you're up to. Where maybe you'll meet a guy you'll like better. That's what scares me! I need you. Come here." He leaned across the space between them and kissed her gently on the forehead.

I was crazy to worry about Karen, about anyone else, Alex thought, as she cuddled close. And she'd exaggerated his anger. For reasons she couldn't begin to understand, Cliff really did love and need her as much as she loved and needed him.

TWO

"**A**lex? That you?" her mother called as soon as she came in the front door. We're in the family room. Come here a minute!"

Alex strode past the living room, as untouched and perfect as a showcase room in a model house, past her father's study, its books and papers just as orderly despite daily use, to the family room, the only place where clutter was allowed.

Her sister bent over a notebook, a pencil covered with bite marks in her mouth.

"Hi, honey." Mrs. Cummings looked up. "How'd the interview go?"

"Pretty well, but the woman I spoke to seems to think I'm a bit young." Alex ran a quick hand over her hair and checked to see if her shirt was well tucked in. She often felt self-conscious around her mom, especially when Kim was near. Kim had their mother's pink-white complexion and green eyes while Alex had her father's build and features. How often she'd heard Kim praised as the good-looking child while she had the "quick mind."

"If you don't get the job this year, you'll get it next, I'm sure," her mother said. "Can you give us a hand here? I forget how to convert fractions into decimals."

Alex moved closer. She bent over Kim's notebook. "Let's see. Oh, sure. All you do is..." She picked up a pencil and began to write.

"It's easy for you!" Kim cried in almost the same tone her mother used when things got beyond her. "Mr. Coe said you were his best student when you were in his class. And I'm just an airhead."

"You're *not* an airhead, and everything's *not* so easy for me!" Alex dropped the pencil. She always hated when her parents called Kim that, even though her mother assured her it was only a joke. It was like they were each given roles to play—the dumb, pretty child and the plain, smart one.

She took in the mess, yesterday's papers still on the end table, the cat in Daddy's chair, new napkins needed in the holder, the flowers in the vase nearly dead. Daddy would be home soon. She got an uneasy feeling in the pit of her stomach. He'd be annoyed.

"Out you go!" She scooped up Nefertiti, scratched the cat's neck, then opened the door and dropped her outside. "Mom, why do you let her sit on Dad's chair? You know how he feels about all the hair!"

"You worry too much, Alex. We'll straighten up

before your father gets home. By the way, Mrs. Taylor phoned. She wants you to call her back."

"Uh-oh!" Alex rushed off to the phone. "I bet she's calling about staying with her kids this summer. I was supposed to call yesterday but I wanted to wait till I heard about the Y job! Darn! I hope there's no problem!"

She could hear the twins fighting in the background when Mrs. Taylor answered.

"Hi, Mrs. Taylor," Alex said. "It's Alex. Sorry I didn't get back to you sooner about the job."

"Nicole!" Mrs. Taylor shouted. "Don't touch that, you hear? Cassidy! Watch your milk!" To Alex she said, "We're having a bit of chaos here. Condition normal."

Alex giggled. "About taking care of Nicole and Cassidy this summer..."

"Yes, that's just what I phoned about. When you didn't call I figured you got that job you wanted so I phoned around and found someone else. Just wanted to let you know."

"Oh!" Alex swallowed her disappointment and tried to sound cheerful. "I hope it works out well for you and the kids. Thanks, anyway. Have a nice summer."

When she hung up she stared out the glass doors to the garden. Her mother spent hours each week tending the flower beds. Now, red and yellow roses lined a sunny wall, their scent strong in the house.

She nibbled around her thumb, thinking. What

would she do all summer? Jobs at the mall would be taken already. She didn't want to go to summer school and she didn't want to just hang out all day. Without plans it would make the hours waiting for Cliff seem endless.

Last summer she'd had Jenna, her best friend, to pass the long, hot days with. They could spend whole afternoons just polishing their nails and browsing through fashion magazines. They'd talk about cute guys and sisters or brothers who got on their nerves, and how little their parents understood them. Jenna. She felt an uncomfortable pang of guilt. Since she and Cliff had started going together she hardly saw her friend. In the last months they probably spoke once and, in fact, Jenna seemed to have new friends now. Still, remembering what fun they used to have, she thought that if Jenna had no summer plans maybe they could do something together.

She grabbed an apple, called out that she'd be back to help straighten up, and hurried down the street.

"Alex!" Jenna exclaimed when she opened the door. The greeting was guarded, even slightly hostile, Alex thought. "Well, *stranger*! I thought you forgot where I live." Jenna wiped her hands on a dish towel.

"So? Can I come in?"

"Sure, but I'm leaving soon to meet Bonnie and Sue."

"Oh. Well, I won't stay long." She followed Jenna

into the familiar house, feeling like a stranger. Jenna had found new friends; it was only natural, but it hurt. Only months ago she couldn't imagine waking up and not sharing the day with her.

Jenna led the way to the kitchen. "I'm baking a pie for Kristen's birthday. Want to help? Double chocolate peanut butter."

"Her favorite," Alex said.

"*You remember...*"

"Please don't be like that, Jenna," she said, reacting to the sarcasm. "I know I deserve it, but honestly, it can't be helped. Cliff takes up all my spare time but you're still my very best friend."

"Some friend! You never call. You never have time to talk or come over. Cliff takes up *all* your time?" Jenna's voice dropped and she turned away, dusting a board with flour and dumping a lump of dough on it. "If you want to be useful, stir the chocolate so it won't burn."

"I'm sorry," Alex said softly. She moved to the stove and picked up a wooden spoon on the counter. "I've missed you. I really have."

Jenna rolled out the dough and began fitting it into a pie pan. "So, what have you been up to?" Her tone was artificially bright. "The only time I see you is at school, in the hall. Where do you hang out these days? Don't you eat lunch anymore? You're never even in the cafeteria."

"Cliff hates the noise and smell, so I make sand-wiches and we eat in his car. It's not just you. I hardly see *anyone* anymore. It's *terrible*!" She stirred the chocolate. Actually, it wasn't at all terrible, but rather quite wonderful, that Cliff wanted so much of her company.

Jenna measured out peanut butter, put it into the microwave and set the timer. "I guess I'm just jealous." She came to Alex's side. "If I had someone like him, I'd want to spend every minute together too. I guess. Except…"

"Except what?" Alex turned off the burner and took the chocolate off the stove. She offered the spoon to Jenna for a lick and took a taste for herself. "Yum, good. Except what?"

"Oh, nothing."

"Come on! Don't do that. You started something, now finish! Except *what*?"

The microwave buzzer sounded and Jenna went to remove the bowl of softened peanut butter. "I've heard some things, that's all. Things about Cliff. But maybe I shouldn't say."

"*What* things?" Alex crossed her arms over her chest and glared at her friend.

Jenna glanced sheepishly at her. "That… he has a terrible temper. That he… gets out of control some-times.…"

"That's mean! Who would say that? Cliff's the sweetest guy I ever met. I know him! Was it Karen? She's just jealous! My goodness! How mean some people can be!"

"Let's not argue. You're probably right!" Jenna said. "Come on. We'll finish this pie and go upstairs. I bought a new shade of eyeshadow that would look great on you!"

Fifteen minutes later Alex followed Jenna back to her room. "Look at this," Jenna chattered. "I got it at Penney's for nine dollars! Isn't it a bargain! And it looks great on. Here, try it!" She held the sweater out to Alex. "And look! I got a new glass dachshund for my collection. *Bonnie* gave it to me! And have you heard this tape? Wait, I'll put it on!"

Alex slipped the sweater over her head and smiled at herself in the mirror. How good it felt to be together again. She had spent so many hours here, comfortable and totally accepted. She could confide anything, even mean thoughts, and Jenna never criticized.

"Hey! That looks great!" Jenna exclaimed, meeting her eyes in the mirror. "Anytime you want to borrow it, just ask!"

Alex smiled. Around Jenna she always felt prettier than she knew herself to be.

After a while they settled in their old positions, cross-legged and facing each other on the bed. Alex told Jenna about the Y interview and how she'd lost the job caring for the Taylor kids. "And now I don't know what I'll do all summer!"

"We can work together!" Jenna said. "I signed up at youth employment. We could team up! You know—housecleaning, weeding, caring for kids! It would be much more fun—just like we used to!"

"Yeah!" Alex clapped her hands. "Only, no weeding. I hate weeding!"

Jenna giggled and hugged her. "Gosh, it's great to see you again! I've missed you! How long can you stay?"

"Cliff's at graduation practice, so he won't come by until after dinner. Another half hour? But what about Sue and Bonnie?"

"A half hour? They'll wait."

They grabbed hands and bounced on the bed as the phone rang.

Jenna reached across Alex and lifted the receiver. "Joe's Pizza!" She covered her mouth to hold back the giggles. "Our special today is five toppings for ten dollars. May I take your order?" She listened. "Oh, Cliff, hi!" The joy went out of her voice.

Alex put a hand to her throat as her pulse leaped.

"She's not here." Jenna grimaced. "All right, so maybe she is, but she's busy. She'll be home in a half hour. You can see her then."

Alex mouthed, "Cliff?"

Jenna nodded and covered the mouthpiece. "He wants you to leave."

"Give me the phone!"

"You said you could stay!"

"Give me the phone!"

Jenna handed the phone over and turned her back.

"Cliff?" Alex held the receiver tightly to her ear.

"Hi, Cone. That Jenna's a creep!"

"How'd you know I was here?"

"Your mother. What are you doing there anyway?"

"Just visiting."

"Listen. Graduation practice ended early and I thought we could get together. I'll pick you up in five minutes."

"Where?"

"At *your* house."

She'd have to leave right now. "Sure. Okay. See you soon."

"Bye, Cone, and tell that creep friend of yours I don't appreciate being told you won't talk to me."

Alex glanced uneasily in Jenna's direction and replaced the phone. She bounced off the bed. "Sorry, Jenna. Gotta go."

"You just got here! We were going to talk about summer plans! Can't you stay just five more minutes?"

"I can't! Cliff hates waiting."

"So what? It would do him good! For heaven's sake. Don't you get time off for good behavior? Get a life!"

She wanted to fly. Her heart had already left and was halfway home, but she made herself pause at the bedroom door and look back. "Come on, Jenna! I thought you understood!"

"I don't. So go. Run. Maybe that's how it is when you're *badly* in love."

"Walk me to the door?"

"You know the way." Jenna sat hunched over the edge of the bed, hands clasped.

"I'll call about our plans for summer, okay? Promise!" Her legs trembled in their eagerness to be gone.

"Sure," Jenna said. She opened and closed a wooden box, not looking at Alex.

"See you!" Alex flew down the hall and out the door, needing to get home before Cliff arrived.

His car was just pulling to the curb in front of her home when she rounded the corner. She ran to it and climbed in beside Cliff. With a big, happy grin he drew her into his arms. "My goodness. I missed you! I hate when I phone your house and you aren't there. I thought you had stuff to do. How come you went to Jenna's?"

"No reason. We were always best friends. I just wanted to see her." She lay back, head against his chin, content.

"So what did you talk about?"

"School. Friends. Summer plans. *You*."

"Me? What *about* me?" His tone was hostile. She touched his lips. "Jenna thinks you're a hunk and that I'm lucky having a boyfriend like you. She's a little envious."

"Oh." He grinned. "I've changed my mind. She's not such a creep after all." He took her hand to his mouth and kissed it. "I only have a few minutes then I gotta run. Maybe we can go for a drive after dinner." He gave her another kiss then leaned across her and opened the car door. "Call you around seven, okay?"

"I'll be here." She got out of the car and leaned low so she could see him through the window. She never got over the pleasure of looking at him, at that strong chin and dark, deep-set eyes, those lips that knew hers so well. Her heart seemed to crowd her ribs and her mouth went dry.

They touched fingers. "Bye, Cone." He mouthed a kiss then drove off down the street. She waved until he couldn't see her then went slowly into the house. She'd given up a half hour with Jenna for five minutes with Cliff. Was it worth it?

Yes!

THREE

She knew by the music that her father was home. As soon as he came home from work he always turned on his CD player. She could usually judge his mood by the music he selected: Mozart when he was happy, Mahler when he wasn't, and other composers for all the in-between moods. Today she heard Beethoven sonatas, which could mean anything from thoughtful to troubled.

When she came through the family room she noted that her father's chair had been vacuumed and the newspapers picked up. Her mother was humming, a good sign. For as long as she remembered, an unspoken rule in the Cummings household was: Keep Daddy happy.

Without asking, she got out the blue place mats and white china and set out the silverware, water glasses, and napkins. She dumped the wilted flowers from the vase on the mantel and went out to the garden for fresh ones, which she arranged in a low bowl and set in the middle of the table. She stood back to see the effect.

Nice. She turned at the sound of footsteps.

"Hi, Dad!" she said brightly.

Her father glanced up from the packet of mail he was checking. "Hello, sweetie."

Kim skipped into the room. "Nefertiti sat in your chair, Daddy!" She covered her mouth with both hands as she realized what she said. "But Alex put her out and Mommy vacuumed!" she added quickly.

"I told you to keep that cat in your room when she's not outdoors, Kim." Her father frowned. "How many times do I have to tell you?"

"It's really hard, Dad," Alex said, moving to stand beside her sister. "We try!"

"I know, but how will Kim ever learn responsibility if she can't keep track of her own pet!"

"Hello, darling!" Mrs. Cummings came in from the kitchen, a casserole in hand. She smiled warmly. "I made lamb curry—hot—the way you like it! Come, sit down."

Mr. Cummings set his mail aside and took his seat at the end of the table. Alex poured water into the glasses, then sat to her father's right and unfolded her napkin. "How's the case going, Dad?" Until her father had eaten, it was always best to stay away from controversy. "Go to trial yet?"

"Next week." Mr. Cummings watched with interest as his wife passed around the dishes. "I'm afraid you won't see much of me for a while. I'll be working late and grabbing meals on the run."

"Is it likely to last long?" Alex asked, more interested in keeping her father's attention away from her than on his answer.

"It's a complicated mess. The environmental group claims..." He was off on a detailed explanation that Alex tuned out after a while. She'd learned to appear interested when her father lectured. All it took was eye contact, an occasional nod, and maybe a question to keep him talking. That left her mind free to think about Cliff.

She once asked her mother how she could stand to listen to all that legal stuff when it was so boring. Her mother had said that if it was important to her husband, then it should be—and *was*—important to her, too. Men had delicate egos. If you wanted to keep them happy, you never forgot that. "Your father has an important job. He's under pressure all day. It's up to me to make home as pleasant and peaceful as possible."

Alex had listened intently. Her parents had a good marriage, she thought. Her mother must know something other women didn't. What Alex learned might help her know how to keep Cliff happy.

"The lamb's just right, Margaret." Mr. Cummings smiled across the table to his wife. "Get the curry at the Indian shop?"

"Of course, dear."

"Good." He leaned back, satisfied, and smiled

around at each of them. "And what have my girls been up to?"

Sharing time is what Alex called this part of the dinner when she described it to Cliff. For her it was always *anxious* time because no matter what she said, she always seemed to fall short. If she got a 98 on a test, her father asked, "What happened to the other two points?"

"He's not being critical," her mother always said. "It's just that he sets very high standards for us all, including himself."

"A perfectionist's not the worst thing in the world," Cliff said when she told him. "From what you say, he's strict but he's not mean. He rules with a loving hand. Now, take my dad." He laughed, humorlessly. "On the other hand, who'd want to?" When she asked why, he said, "Let's just say he's got a firm *un*loving hand."

Mr. Cummings looked around the table. "Who wants to share first? Alex?"

"Me, Daddy!" Kim bubbled, bouncing up and down in her seat. "Oh, me! Let me!"

"Sure, Kimmy. You first."

"Well..." Alex smiled at the pink flush of excitement on her sister's face. "We're doing a rain forest project at school. My job is to tell about the animals that live there. You know—monkeys and wild boars and stuff!"

"Sounds interesting, sugar. Check the library. Should be some good books on the subject."

Kim nodded and rushed on. "I went to ballet class, and we're putting on a—recital! And I'm going to be a fairy!"

"I know, sweetheart. You told me last week."

"It's just a small part, Martin, but remember, it's her first year," Mrs. Cummings said.

"Ms. De Prima says it's *important*, Daddy!"

"It *is* important, Kim!" Alex reassured her when she heard the anxiety in her sister's voice.

"Sure it is, Kimmy, and I bet you'll make a wonderful fairy," her father said.

"It's next month, on the eighth, Martin," her mother said softly. "The recital. Do you think—"

"I doubt it. You know the trial's next month. You know how busy I am! How can I promise?"

"Oh, yes, of course. I forgot!" Her mother smiled with false brightness. "Kim, darling, listen. If Daddy can't make it, we'll videotape it and show it to him later!"

"It'll be even better that way," her father added, "because then we can see it over and over. Now, Kim! Don't pout! It's ugly. And Alex! You're slouching; sit up like a lady!"

Alex took her hands off the table and sat straighter.

"How about *your* day, honey?"

Alex twisted her hands in her lap. She told about school, about the Y interview and the small chance she'd get the job. She explained how Mrs. Taylor had hired someone else and that she and Jenna might be able to work together.

"You should have called Mrs. Taylor when you said you would, then you wouldn't be in this—pickle." Her father frowned. "Still, you're trying; that's good. If you can't get something, maybe we can find work for you at the office. Would you like that?"

"Oh, Martin! That would be great!" her mother exclaimed. "Wouldn't it, Alex?"

No, it wouldn't. She'd be under her father's critical eye all summer. All the people working at his law office were old. The work would be boring.

Her parents were waiting for an answer. "Thanks, Dad. I'll keep it in mind." She started clearing the dishes. "Cliff's coming over. May I be excused?"

"Again? You're too young to be going steady. Aren't you seeing too much of that boy?"

"I'm not too young!"

"It's okay, Martin, really. It's quite normal for girls her age to go steady. It's flattering, actually, considering—"

Alex looked down at her hands. She knew exactly how her mother intended to finish that sentence: "—considering Alex isn't the prettiest girl he could have."

"He's almost eighteen, isn't he? What's he doing dating a girl almost three years younger?"

"He likes Alex, Martin. Age has nothing to do with it!"

Oh, God, Alex worried. *He's not going to let me go.* She stood by the table, plates in hand, waiting, trying to appear unconcerned. Mom, the intermediary, was on her side.

"He's a very nice young man, Martin. A real gentleman," Mrs. Cummings went on. "They're good kids. Don't worry!"

Her father hesitated, then said, "Oh, all right. But no later than ten!"

"Dad!" Alex protested. "It only gives us an hour!" She clamped her mouth shut at her mother's warning look. "Yes, Dad," she said, hurrying out of the room before he could change his mind. "I'll be home by ten."

FOUR

"**W**hat's wrong, Cliff?"

Alex asked as soon as she got into the car beside him. She took his hand and touched it to her cheek.

"Nothing!" He yanked his hand away and slammed it on the steering wheel. "Everything!" He thrust the key in the ignition and took off down the street with a squeal of rubber.

Alex pressed her back against the seat and braked her feet hard on the floor. "Please, Cliff. Slow down!" she begged.

"Shut up! Don't tell me what to do!"

She clenched her hands and stared ahead at the trees and houses flying by. Cliff never talked to her like that. Well, almost never. What could have happened to upset him so? When she glanced his way he sat almost rigid over the wheel, still with fury.

"Talk about *your* father! You don't know how well off you are!" he said after a time. "Mom's scared to open her mouth to *my* dad, never knows what'll set him off so he'll haul off and swat her good!"

"He *hits* her?" Alex asked, astonished.

"You bet! And he gets on Diane's case so often I wouldn't be the least surprised if she took off. *Now* he's after me!"

"*Why*, Cliff?" She turned to watch him.

"He doesn't need a reason!" Cliff took his eyes from the road and glared at Alex. "He's after me about college. It's not good enough I've been accepted. He says I should know what I'll major in or I'll just waste his money. How should I know what I want to be? Isn't that what college is for?"

"What about science? You're good at math and stuff. Could you major in that, maybe?" Alex's voice faltered.

"Now *you're* telling me what to do? I don't have enough bosses at home?"

"I didn't mean... I thought—"

"Just let me do the thinking, okay? It's *my* life!" He jammed on the brakes. "Dumb driver! Did you see what he did? Cut right in front of me!"

"Yes, but Cliff, he—"

"He *what*?"

"Nothing." She looked away. The *dumb* driver had signaled for at least a mile that he wanted to pass. Cliff had ignored him and even deliberately stopped him from moving into their lane. She supposed the driver could have fallen back and pulled in behind, as Cliff wanted, so Cliff probably was right. "Honey," she said, trying to calm him. "Let's stop at the drive-in. I bet you hardly ate dinner if your dad was on the warpath like that."

He threw her a grateful look. "You're right. I'm starved. Gee, Cone, I'm sorry. I shouldn't take it out on you. You, of all people. But you just can't imagine how it is at home. Sometimes it gets so bad I could... I don't know!" He shook his head. "Don't ever give up on me. I couldn't get along without you."

"Relax," she said, kneading the knots in his tense shoulders with one hand. "It's okay." She loved the feeling she got helping Cliff. He needed someone to unload on and though his sudden fury sometimes made her stomach ache, she could take it. He never meant to hurt *her*.

"Aaah. That feels good. Sooo good!" Cliff purred as she massaged his neck. "You are *marvelous*!" He switched on the radio and punched the button for his favorite station. The music came on loud and strong— so loud that Alex reached to turn it lower.

"Don't!" Cliff grabbed her hand.

"Oh, okay!" If he wanted the music loud, fine. After what had happened at home he deserved special consideration. She kept one hand on his neck, smiling. Look how she'd managed to lift him out of that bad mood.

She was home by ten, just as her father had ordered, and went straight to her room. For the next half hour she sat on her bed with a book of short stories in her lap. She'd read the book once already, for pleasure, and settled on one particular story with a mind to retelling it. How could she describe the setting? Did she really understand how the viewpoint character felt so she could make the listener care? What kind of body language would a girl like the one in the story use?

When the phone rang she dropped her book and grabbed the receiver before it could ring a second time. Cliff always phoned before eleven, even if they'd just said good night.

"My midnight caller," she whispered into the phone, cradling it against her cheek. "My love fix."

Cliff's soft chuckle came across the wire. "What if it was someone else?"

She laughed, imagining what a stranger would think being greeted like that.

"What are you doing, ice-cream Cone?"

She smiled at his gentleness. "Reading stories. Trying to decide which one to work on."

"School's nearly over. Who would you perform for? Besides, isn't that kind of kid stuff?"

"Why?" His put-down hurt.

"How many grown-ups pretend they're characters in a story? Don't you like being you? Must you always try to be someone else? I like *you*, not the pretend yous."

"You *know* the real me. Gosh, Cliff," she added lamely, "I thought you liked hearing me tell stories."

"Sure, but not if it cuts into *our* time together."

"But it doesn't! I was just—"

"Let's not argue. How'd you do on the Spanish test?"

She hesitated for a second, shifting mental gears. "Spanish? Oh. I got ninety-six."

"Ninety-six! What happened to the other four points?" He chuckled, knowing that's what her father would say, then added. "Ninety-six is great. I'm proud of you. Know what I'd like to do to you right now?"

Alex blushed and closed her eyes. "What?"

"Guess."

An excited tingle went down her spine. "Tell me."

He lowered his voice to a hoarse whisper. "First, I'd like to kiss the tip of your... pretty nose."

She winced at the reference to her worst feature. How could he praise a nose like hers? She waited, almost holding her breath for what he'd say next.

"Then... I'd like to kiss your—"

The hall chimes began sounding.

"Better hurry!" she teased. "It's almost witching hour and you know what happens if we talk one minute past eleven!"

"And then... I'd like to kiss your neck and then your..." He rushed hurriedly down her body until the ninth tone.

Her face felt hot. "I love you, Cliff," she said. "See you tomorrow."

"Night, Cone, love. Sleep tight."

The eleventh chime sounded and Cliff hung up. Before replacing the receiver, she held it against her cheek and closed her eyes, smiling. Then she buried her face in the pillow and giggled her joy. If for some reason Cliff didn't call one night, she went crazy. She'd imagine all kinds of terrible things. He'd been in an accident. He'd forgotten. He was punishing her for something she'd said or hadn't said. Or worst of all, he didn't love her anymore. But he did phone, every night. He did love her.

Now, she could go to sleep content.

FIVE

"**M**om, Dad," Cliff said. "This is Alex, my girlfriend."

It was a hot, sunny day and the graduates, with their relatives and friends, were gathering on the football field just before the ceremony. Alex forced a stiff, scared smile. She wanted very much for Cliff's parents to like her. She felt pretty in her new summer dress. Her straight, limp hair had curled softly from the humidity and looked as good as it ever could.

Mr. Vandermeer held out a hand. Tall and distinguished, he had a smile like Cliff's. She found it hard to imagine him being someone to fear or hate. "Nice to meet you, dear." His eyes swept over her and returned to her face with a look that brought an unexpected flush to Alex's face.

"I hear you're a marvelous storyteller," Mrs. Vandermeer said. She was a delicate woman, elegantly dressed.

Alexandra glanced in surprise at Cliff, aware that his

father was still watching her. Flustered, she turned to Cliff's sister. "Hi, Diane."

She could be so pretty, Alex had thought when they met before. Her eyes were a bright blue yet she always kept them averted. She wore dull colors, oversize clothes, almost as if she was trying to hide herself.

"Diane? Didn't you hear Alex? Answer her!" Mr. Vandermeer said.

Diane darted a defiant glance at her father, then in a voice barely audible said, "Hi."

"Will you excuse us a minute?" Cliff's father seemed to be looking over Alex's shoulder. "There's someone we must see." He brushed Alex, in passing, as he led his wife away.

Alex shivered.

"Wait!" Cliff stretched a hand out, then withdrew it. "Oh, well, doesn't matter," he muttered as they disappeared in the crowd.

"What did you expect, Cliff?" Diane asked with unexpected vehemence. "You know Dad. There's always someone who's more important than his family."

"Don't start things, Di! Things were going so well. Don't ruin it!" Cliff said.

A light flashed in Diane's blue eyes, then died. She folded her hands in front of her in a demure, submissive pose.

"Doesn't Cliff look great in his cap and gown?" Alex asked, eager to ease the strain.

"Yeah," Diane said.

"I hope they'll be back so you can all sit together." Cliff fanned himself with his mortarboard and tried to see where his parents had gone.

"Maybe we should find seats," Alex said. "The stands are filling up."

"Right. I better get going, too. They're lining up for the graduation march." Cliff gave Alex a quick kiss. "See you later, Cone."

"Look! There's Jenna!" Alex said just as he was turning away. "Come on, Diane. She's a good friend. Let's find seats with her!"

"No!" Cliff swung around.

"Why?"

"Because—it's *my* graduation and I don't want her around."

"But..." Her voice faltered at the look on Cliff's face. "All right. Where would you like us to sit?" She saw Jenna slip away in the crowd.

"With my parents."

"Oh!" So that was it! He didn't want Jenna around only because he saw this occasion as "family" only, including *her*. "See you later, then," she said, smiling.

She led the way up into the bleachers looking for the Vandermeers and for enough seats so they could all sit together. Up high she had a good view and saw Cliff's parents below. She stood and when Mr. Vandermeer saw her, waved with both hands.

"You're wasting your time," Diane said. "They won't sit with us."

"Oh?"

"They won't! See? I told you!"

The Vandermeers took seats next to the couple they'd been talking to. There were no spaces beside them.

"I guess your mom didn't want to climb way up here in those high heels," Alex said.

"Mom would climb Mount Everest in high heels if Dad said to!" Diane said. She stared straight ahead, hugging herself like she was cold.

Poor Diane. So full of hate. Every word a barb. She wanted to like her for Cliff's sake, but it was hard. As for his parents, it really wasn't right for them to have abandoned Diane and her, but did it really matter?

Alex's attention soon shifted to the field below. The seniors, in caps and gowns, began their march across the grass to white wooden chairs in front of a raised platform. Alex strained to see Cliff but from the distance everyone looked the same.

The band played selections from Sousa. The principal spoke. The honored guest spoke. The valedictorian spoke, and then there were endless awards. Sitting in the hot sun, Alex began to feel sleepy. Then suddenly, she jolted awake.

"The award for best all-around athlete goes to..." The athletic coach paused for dramatic effect. "Clifford Vandermeer!"

Alex gasped and covered her mouth to stifle an excited scream. Cliff's classmates leaped to their feet, applauding and shouting as they had for some of the other award winners. Cliff left his seat and made his way to the aisle and down the grass to the podium. "Look at him!" Alex shouted, glancing at Diane. "Isn't he great! Aren't you proud? *Everyone* loves him!"

Diane clapped hard, face flushed. "Thank God."

"Huh?" Alex glanced quickly at Cliff's sister.

"*Dad* won best athlete in high school. If Cliff hadn't won, he'd never hear the end of it. That's my *father*!"

"Oh, Diane!" Alex frowned, still applauding as Cliff walked off, trophy high, glancing up into the stands.

The ceremony ended soon after and visitors spilled out of the stands onto the field. Seniors milled about congratulating each other, searching for their families and friends, hugging and smiling and taking pictures. Alex pushed through the crowds looking for Cliff and his parents.

"Wow! I never expected!" Cliff exclaimed when they found him. He held the trophy out for them to see. "I mean, there were plenty of better guys..."

"*You're* the best! You are! Everyone thinks so!" Alex cried, rushing to hug him.

"Where are the folks?" Cliff held one hand over his eyes to block out the sun and searched the crowd. "Didn't you sit together?"

"Hey, you didn't really think we would, did you?" Diane asked.

"Here they come now," Alex said.

"Well, Cliff!" Mr. Vandermeer said. "You did it, just like the old man! Let's see that thing!" He took the trophy, examined it, nodded, and gave it back. "Not bad. We'll put it next to mine. Proves you're a *man*."

"Not hardly," Diane said softly.

"*Diane*!"

Alex drew in her breath and Diane stepped closer to Cliff at her father's threatening tone. Had he intended to strike her? Before she could decide, Karen burst into their midst. "Cliff! At last! I've been looking all over for you. Hi, Mr. and Mrs. Vandermeer. Hi, guys!" She lifted a camera from around her neck and handed it to Alex. "Would you mind? I'm getting pictures of all my old buddies so I can blackmail them at our tenth reunion!" She laughed, tucked an arm around Cliff's waist, and leaned her head against his shoulder. "Say cheese, hunk," she said between clamped teeth.

"Cheese." Cliff rolled his eyes at Alex, but didn't pull away.

Alex stepped back, caught them in the viewfinder, and quickly snapped the picture. "Here."

"Thanks." Karen took back her camera. "Well, I'll be off! Congratulations, Cliff! Bye, everyone! Hey, Trevor! Wait up!" she called, hurrying away.

"They sure fall hard for you, don't they Cliff?" Diane said.

Alex sensed the sudden tension as Cliff stepped between his father and Diane. "She didn't mean anything, Dad. Let's go, huh? We've got reservations at the Atheneum. Cone?" He pressed Diane forward and took Alex's arm.

"But—"

"It's okay, Alex," Cliff whispered. "We'll get pictures later. Dad's in one of his moods."

She awoke early Monday morning as if it was a school day and nearly leaped out of bed to be ready for when Cliff came by, but it wasn't a school day. It was the first day of vacation and Cliff would already be at the Y. She lay in bed listening to the doves in the pine tree outside her window, to a dog barking off in the distance, to her mother and father's voices murmuring downstairs.

By now Cliff would be greeting the little kids brought in by their moms and dads. She could imagine him in white shorts, with his hairy legs, and Y-camp shirt, moving among the kids, calming a crying child, showing a boy how to throw a ball, explaining a game. She smiled to herself. He had so much to give.

How would *she* spend the long day before she could see Cliff? Just lying about and feeling bad would make the day endless. No. She'd phone Jenna. They'd go down to youth employment and sign up. They'd go through their lists of families with kids and call each one. Maybe they could start a day care. Between them they could handle maybe six or eight kids. Take them for walks, to the park, the zoo...

Or they could draw up flyers, offering to put on birthday parties. They'd have themes, Indians maybe. Pirates. They'd create headdresses and hats for each child. She'd tell stories. The more she thought about it the more excited she became.

She heard the phone ring as she left the shower and started to dress but thought nothing of it until Kim burst into the room. "Hurry! It's a lady from the Y on the phone, Alex! Maybe you got the job! Hurry, she's waiting!"

In a flurry of hope, Alex yanked her T-shirt over wet hair and ran barefoot to the hall phone. She took a deep, scared breath and picked up the receiver. "Hello?"

She heard a click as her mother hung up the extension.

"Alexandra?"

"Yes."

"This is Ms. Wilson. I have some good news. How'd you like to start working for us today?"

"Oh, gosh! You mean it? Today? Oh, yes, *yes*! I'd love to!"

"Well then, how soon can you get here?"

"I need a ride. Just a minute. I'll check with my mom."

Two minutes later she was back on the phone, slightly out of breath. "Ms. Wilson?" she cried. "No problem. I can be there in fifteen minutes, a half hour tops." She could hardly control her delight. "And Ms. Wilson? Thanks! Thanks a lot!"

But now what about Jenna and the plans they had made? Could she work at the Y and still do things with her?

SIX

Ms. Wilson said she could fill out the paperwork later. The children were across the courtyard, upstairs. "Just introduce yourself to Brian; he's head counselor. He'll tell you what to do," she said.

Alex ran across the courtyard and up the stairs. She could hardly wait to start. Wouldn't Cliff be surprised to see her!

Even before opening the door, she heard the children's voices. "Itsy Bitsy Spider, went up the water spout…" She smiled. It was a song she used often with small children she baby-sat.

She pushed the door open and stepped into a large room with shelves for clothes and lunches, work tables and chairs, and big colorful pictures on the walls. A blackboard listed children's names—Krista, Becky, Robin, Eric, Caitlin, Michael, Darcy, Lori… The kids sat in rows on the floor according to age, singing as loud as they could. Counselors sat with them, or stood around the sides. She recognized some of them—seniors or first-year college students—and hesitated, not sure where to turn.

Facing her, directing the singing, was Karen. Her face, her whole body, radiated enthusiasm and energy. "Again!" she cried, cupping a hand to one ear as if she couldn't hear. The children sang even louder.

Cliff hurried over, a pleased expression on his face. "What are you doing here, Alex? They don't like friends dropping by."

"I'm not just dropping by. Ms. Wilson called. I got the job!"

"You *did*? Hey!"

She wanted to hug him, he seemed so delighted. Instead, she just stood there, foolishly grinning until she finally remembered what she came for. "Who's Brian? I'm supposed to check in with him."

"He's that tall guy at the desk. Come on. I'll introduce you." He took her arm and walked her to the far corner of the room, where a pleasant-looking young man wearing jeans and a Y T-shirt was trying to fix a jammed audio tape machine.

"Brian, this is Alex Cummings. Our new counselor."

Brian put down the screwdriver, stood up, and offered his hand. "Hi, Alex. Sure glad to see you. Ms. Wilson said you'd be coming. We're really short-handed. I'm putting you with the younger children, the

K through third. Karen's got *eighteen* of them, which is more than a handful. Hope you have eyes in the back of your head! Ever done this kind of thing before?"

"I've taken care of lots of little kids, but never been a counselor."

"No sweat. Karen will show you the ropes; I'm sure you'll catch on fast. The idea is to keep the kids busy and happy, help them build skills and self-confidence. The hardest part is the noise. Drives me nuts. Know what I mean?" He crossed his eyes.

Alex smiled.

"Here's the week's schedule. Any questions, just ask. We're all here to help."

Alex glanced at the sheet he handed her. Every forty-five minutes some new activity was listed. Snack time came next.

"Karen's just finishing the group sing," Brian said as the children belted out the Y-camp song. "Why don't you and Cliff go bring up the refreshments."

"He likes you," Cliff said as they left the room and ran down the stairs together.

"I'm glad! I liked him, too!"

"Just don't like him *too* much!"

Alex giggled and grabbed Cliff's hand. "Isn't it a miracle, my getting the job at the last minute? I'm so happy, I could dance. Come dance with me!"

Cliff laughed and squeezed her hand.

One of the adult staff came out of the main building and looked their way. "Uh-oh!" Alex exclaimed, moving away. "Better not. Not during work hours! But won't it be great being together? And aren't those little kids *cute!* Where do we go for the refreshments? Oh, goodness! Listen to me. I'm babbling!"

"The kitchen's in there." Cliff crossed the courtyard and opened a door for her. They went into a large, poorly lit room smelling of sugar and cinnamon. He drew her across the tiled floor, beyond work counters, an oven, stove and refrigerator, to a dark corner. "This is what I felt like doing the minute you came into the room," he whispered. He pressed her against the wall, pulled her close, and gave her a long, loving kiss.

"Cliff!" she whispered, startled by the sudden hum of the refrigerator. "Not now! Not here. What if someone comes?"

"It's okay, don't worry. We're alone, and we'd hear them."

"But Brian said…"

"*Forget* Brian!"

"I feel funny, Cliff. Really. It'll look bad if—"

"All *right*!" Cliff let her go. "Geez, am I sick of his name! Brian, Brian! All you hear all day. You'd think he was the almighty! But okay. He'll probably send a posse if we don't get back soon, so let's go."

In a few minutes, loaded with gallon jugs of punch, the crackers and toweling, they went back upstairs, but Cliff hurried ahead, no longer playful.

"Don't be angry," she said, as they ran up the last few steps. "We'll have time alone after work."

"I'm *not* angry. Geez!" Cliff opened the door to the noisy playroom. The floor vibrated with children stomping around as elephants, lions, and tigers. He deposited the heavy punch bottles on a table, turned, and jogged across the room to his own group.

"Bye," she called after him, but he didn't answer. She left her supplies on the table and went to help Karen.

"Oh, boy! Am I glad to see you!" Karen said, pushing a strand of hair from her eyes. She was organizing the eighteen youngest children into a line. "If you'll tear the paper towels into squares and give each kid one, plus a graham cracker, I'll pour the drinks, okay? We'll talk later... and *thanks*, oh, thanks for coming! Elliot! Don't push!" she called out.

For the rest of the morning Alex found herself too busy to think about or even look for Cliff. Following snacks, she helped the children do sponge painting and then took them outdoors to play ball. Sorting out the children assigned to her, learning their names, and getting a sense of their needs took all her attention. Most disquieting was that Brian always seemed to be near, watching. What if he didn't like how she dealt with the children?

At lunchtime, she led her group outdoors with their lunch bags and boxes. They settled with Karen's group under a large, shady oak. Alex moved among the children, helping unscrew thermoses and showing them how to tear open their plastic-wrapped cookies. Finally, she sat on the ground near Karen to eat the lunch she'd hurriedly fixed before leaving home.

"So what do you think?" Karen asked.

Alex leaned her head against the tree and closed her eyes. "I didn't realize it would be so hard. By five I'll be deaf. My ears are still ringing from the last Y-camp cheer. And Brian makes me nervous. I seem to drop things or bump into tables just because I know he's watching."

Karen nodded. "Don't worry. As soon as he trusts you, he won't be around so much. And as for fatigue, you'll get used to that. The first few days of summer camp always wear me out." She opened a bag of carrot sticks and nibbled one thoughtfully. "You'll want to get to know your kids. I already know most of mine from working day care after school. Some of them are away from home eight in the morning until sometimes as late as six when a parent comes to pick them up."

"That's a long stretch for such little kids," Alex said.

"Yeah. But lots of parents work these days, or it's a single parent thing. What choice do they have?"

Alex's eyes wandered around the field as they spoke. Each group of ten children sat with a counselor somewhere on the grass. The air smelled sweet, and a squirrel scurried up a tree. Off to the left Cliff leaned against a picnic table surrounded by third- and fourth-graders. She caught his eye and gave a "Hi" sign. He waved back.

"Uh-oh!" she exclaimed as her attention returned to the children. Karen had warned her about Justin. Smaller than the others, he was a loner who tended to wander off to the parking lot, looking for his mother. The child had just spilled his milk. He held his wet T-shirt away from his skin and stared in horror at himself. Alex grabbed a wad of paper toweling and jumped to her feet.

"It's all right, Justin. Come on, sweetie. Let's go change your clothes," Alex said, but the boy scrambled to his feet and ran.

"Justin, wait!" Alex called, chasing after him. He darted about like a balloon with its air rushing out. Her first day and she couldn't solve a simple problem. Everyone was watching. What would Brian think? "Justin, stop! Please, come back!"

Suddenly Brian rushed by. "Hey, little guy!" He caught the small boy and squatted down to eye level, holding his shoulders. "What's the hurry? Where are you going?" He looked up at Alex. "What happened?"

"He spilled his milk, that's all. I just wanted to get him into something dry." Alex touched Justin's head. "Come on, sweetie. You must be cold in that wet shirt. Let's go inside and change."

Justin clung to Brian.

"I don't want to force him," Alex said. "He needs time to feel safe with me."

"Let's go inside together," Brian said. "Just you, me, and Alexandra. Okay?" To show his confidence in Alex, he put an arm around her shoulder.

Alex took the child's hand. It was cold and clammy. His face was streaked with dirty tears. Maybe this was his first camp experience, she thought. Maybe he was just terribly shy.

"Okay, kiddo," Brian said, when they came indoors. He bent again to eye level. "Alexandra's going to fix you good as new. *Alexandra* will do it, not me! She's your counselor. See you later, alligator." He winked at Alex and took off.

Alex found the child's hooded jacket and took him to the restroom where she pulled off his milk-soaked shirt and dried his chest. "When I was your age I used to spill things all the time," she said as she worked. "Orange juice and milk, snow cones and ice cream... Goodness. I was so clumsy they called me Miss Klutz." She pretended a great sadness, then giggled.

Justin watched her warily.

"You're not afraid of *me*, are you, Justin?" She zipped his jacket. "You think I'm going to eat you up?" She dropped her voice and with a grin said, "Gobble, gobble, yum, yum! Such a tasty little boy!"

Justin managed a tentative smile and she hugged

him. "It's okay to make mistakes. Everyone does."

Justin plugged a thumb in his mouth and nodded.

"Now let's go back outside and finish lunch. This afternoon we're going to the park! I bet you can swing higher than a bird!"

Justin took his thumb out long enough to say, "I can pump myself!"

"I bet you can," she said. "I bet you really can!"

At a quarter of five Alex scurried about sorting lunchboxes and clothes for the children being picked up at five. "Don't forget your shirt, Justin." She handed the damp T-shirt to him in a plastic bag and helped zip up his jacket. He stayed at her side while she tended to other children, then led them to the field where parents would pick them up.

He clung to her until his mother appeared, and then, without a glance, ran off.

"Bye!" Alex called. "See you tomorrow!"

She turned back to the classrooms, eased her tense shoulders, took a deep breath, and thought for the first time in hours about Cliff. Now, they'd drive to the lake and talk about the day. There was so much to share. Maybe he had some ideas about how to help Justin feel more secure. She wanted to know how his day went, too.

"Got a ride?" Karen asked after they'd cleaned up and gotten the supplies together for the next day. She hoisted her day pack and checked her watch.

"Cliff's taking me home," Alex said.

"You sure? Brian collared him a bit ago. Looked like they had words. Cliff seemed pretty unhappy. I think he left."

"Oh no; that's impossible. He said he'd drive me. Maybe he went to the restroom or the office or something. He'll be by."

"Want to check? I'll wait."

"No, you go on. I'm sure he's around. He wouldn't go home without me."

"Don't count on it."

Alex frowned.

"Sorry," Karen said. "Maybe he's changed. I'll tootle along, then. See you tomorrow." She left the room, humming "Itsy Bitsy Spider."

The silence, after so much noise, made her uneasy. Was it possible Cliff would leave without her? No!

For a while she ambled around the room, checking the time every minute. She walked down the hall to where the older children sometimes played. The room was empty. Growing panicky, she hurried across the yard to see if Cliff's car was still in the back lot. Only one car remained, an old, gray Toyota.

Maybe he went to get gas, she reasoned, or maybe he reparked to go to the office. She ran back and through the main building of the Y, almost empty at this late time of day, to look out at the front parking lot. No red Mustang. She felt tears building in her throat. What was going on? Could he have left, knowing she was still here, waiting? Why? Did something happen? Was he sick? An emergency at home? But wouldn't he have left a message?

What was going on?

SEVEN

"**I** thought Cliff would bring you home," her mother said when she came for Alex.

Alex climbed into the car, too upset to speak, and her mother pulled out of the parking lot into traffic.

"Well, what happened?"

"He had to leave. A... dental appointment," she lied.

"Oh. Is he picking you up tomorrow or do I have to drive you?"

"I... I'm not sure."

"Something wrong?" Mrs. Cummings glanced quickly at Alex.

"No, Mom, I'm just tired."

"So how did it go?"

She tried to bring enthusiasm to her voice, but the day, which had begun with such excitement and promise, had lost its luster. There had to be a reason for Cliff's odd behavior. Something he couldn't control. Or had she misunderstood? Had he said anything about *not* picking her up? She longed to be home so she could close herself in her room and call him.

Diane answered the phone. "Oh hi," she said in her usual expressionless voice. "Yeah, he just came in. Cliff? Cliff? For you!"

Alex's heart beat hard and fast while she waited what seemed ages before Cliff picked up the receiver.

"Yes?"

"Cliff, it's me!"

"Yes?"

Yes? Yes? Is that all he has to say? "What happened to you today? Where were you? Are you sick? Why didn't you pick me up?" She couldn't keep the hurt from her voice. "I thought we were supposed to go home together!"

"After the way you acted?"

"After the way... ? What are you *talking* about?"

"Come on, Alex. *You* know. You *must* know!"

She searched her mind. Was it because she didn't want to make out in the Y kitchen? Had she said something to hurt him? Karen said Cliff and Brian had had "words." Might it have to do with that? Confused and frustrated, she cried, "I don't know what you mean! You're scaring me! Tell me. Why are you angry?"

"Come on, Alexandra! You don't think I'm that dense! You suppose I didn't notice that stuff between you and Brian?"

"Me and Brian?" she squeeked. "What stuff?"

"Don't tell me you don't know when you're coming on to someone. It was *very* obvious! Everyone saw it. You made a fool of me."

"What?"

"Don't give me the innocent act. I saw the way you flirted with him, the way he came on to you with his hand on your shoulder and all that. I saw when the two of you walked off together with that little kid. How he hung around you all afternoon. You encouraged him! You liked it. You *tried* to keep him there! What were you trying to do? Make me jealous?"

"But, but—that's not true!"

"Alex! I'm *not* blind!"

"Brian hung around because I'm new, and he's checking on me. That's all there is to it!" She heard a shrillness in her voice that was desperation. How could he see things so different from the way they were?

Suddenly it hit her. He was scared, scared to lose her. He loved her so much he couldn't bear her even talking to another boy. She hadn't thought he even noticed, yet he'd been watching all the time—misreading, out of his own insecurity, what went on with Brian. That's why he'd left her at the Y—to teach her a lesson. She should have realized how Cliff might feel and been more careful!

Looking at it this way, she was touched, even flattered. If *he'd* been with another girl maybe she'd have tried to hurt him somehow too.

No she wouldn't. She couldn't.

"I'm sorry you misunderstood," she said, calmer now. "Honestly, Cliff—I swear, I'm innocent. Justin—the little boy—was afraid of me. I don't know why. Brian thought if he went inside with us, it would calm him. Maybe he put a hand on my shoulder to show he trusted me. Brian's hanging around because I'm new. He's not sure I can be trusted yet. Karen even said so. Please, Cliff. That's all there was to it. Believe me!"

"Humph…" She heard the first flicker of doubt in Cliff's voice. "I still don't like it."

"Karen said you and Brian had words. What about?"

"Nothing."

"Oh, come on. Tell me!"

"He read me the riot act over how I handled one of the kids—and I didn't deserve it. I didn't *shake* the kid like he said!"

She could hear Cliff's anger building again so she switched the subject. "Look. In the future if Brian tries to talk to me I'll be as cold as… as an ice cube! As… as… the polar ice cap!"

"Humph," Cliff repeated, but with a smile in his voice.

"Okay?" She held her breath, waiting.

"Okay." Cliff finally agreed.

The knot in her stomach relaxed. "And don't ever leave me stranded like today!"

"Then stay away from Brian and don't come on to other guys!"

"I didn't—" She stopped herself. "I won't! Promise!" She wondered about *his* argument with Brian but thought it best not to ask more. "We're going out for pizza in a few minutes. Dad's working late. Want to come?"

"If we can get away afterward and go off by ourselves, like we *couldn't* do this afternoon."

"Sure." A shiver of pleasure went through her.

"See you soon then, Cone. Bye."

She hung up and sighed with relief. He hadn't called her Alexandra or Alex—but Cone. She was forgiven.

"Just look at him, the way he handles Kim," Mrs. Cummings said, nudging Alex as they headed into the pizza parlor. "Treats her like an adult. Isn't it cute!"

Cliff walked ahead of them, holding her sister's hand and listening intently to her conversation. Kim adored Cliff, but then, who didn't?

Alex skipped ahead and linked an arm through Cliff's. "This boy on my block is always doing mean things to me," Kim was saying. "Today, he chased me!"

"He probably likes you," Cliff said.

"No, he hates me. I told him if he didn't stop I'd get my sister's boyfriend to punch him out."

"You did, huh?" Cliff was amused. "Is he bigger than me?"

"He's big! The biggest boy in fourth grade! But you're bigger. Cliff, will you?"

"Leave Cliff alone, Kim," Alex said. "He's had

enough with little kids pestering him all day."

"That's all right. I don't mind." Cliff put an arm around Kim.

A high school friend came out of the building. "Hi, Cliff, Alex," he greeted. "How's it going? Who's your little friend?"

"My new girlfriend," Cliff said, all seriousness. "Kim Cummings."

Kim giggled and smiled back at her mother. Cliff was in such a good mood now he was even romancing Kim.

"How do you do, Kim. I'm Roger. If you ever tire of this hunk, let me know." He winked at Cliff and went on to his car.

"Did you hear that, Alex?" Kim whispered as they walked into the pizza parlor. "He thought I was Cliff's girlfriend!"

"Well, you *are*!" Cliff tousled her hair. "My number two girlfriend."

"Who's number one?"

"Alex, of course!"

Alex leaned toward Cliff and bumped him happily and then walked ahead to hold an empty table.

"What do you say we order a large vegetarian pizza?" Mrs. Cummings asked, studying the menu. "No pepperoni, no anchovies. Just cheese and veggies. How about it?"

"I don't believe this!" Alex addressed Cliff. "She

never wants vegetarian pizza. She always wants pepperoni when we come with Dad!"

"That's your father's favorite, not mine," her mother
said.

"I'm for the large, with *everything* on it." Cliff put
an arm around Kim. "How about you, peanut?"

"Sounds good to me."

"Alex?"

Alex made a face. "It's got so much *junk* on it..."

"Poor baby. Never can make up her mind." Cliff
bent over, kissed Alex on the cheek, then got up. "I'll
decide, okay?" He was off to the counter to order.

Alex grinned sheepishly. "Cliff always decides for us,
sort of like Daddy does. Except he knows I get indiges-
tion from green peppers and olives but he gets them anyway, because *he* loves them and I don't mind. I just take
off all the stuff I can't eat and give them to him."

Her mother nodded. She passed napkins around for
each of them. "It's just not worth fussing about most
things if you want to keep the peace with a man. Your
father has strong likes and dislikes. There's nothing
wrong with trying to please him when I can."

When *she* married, Alex thought, she'd want someone like her dad. She was never afraid of him the way
Diane was of her father. Yes, he was demanding sometimes, maybe too critical, but he loved them, and what
he said counted most. Old-fashioned, maybe by today's
standards, but it worked in keeping the family strong.

Cliff had lots of qualities like Dad. He was strong willed and dominant, but very loving.

"What if you thought Dad *wasn't* right? Would you say anything?" Alex leaned forward, eyes intent on her mother's face.

"Oh sure, I'd speak up. Your father's a reasonable man and there are ways to get what you want without being pushy. An iron hand in a silk glove—you know." Mrs. Cummings smiled impishly. "Of course, your dad is very bright and wise, too. In the end, what he says goes. Kim! Leave the sugar alone!"

Alex gazed around the large, noisy room, letting her mother's words sink in. She'd heard variations of the same theme many times before and listened hard. Her mother seemed to have the secret for keeping her father happy, a secret Alex was eager to learn. Having a boyfriend was terribly important in high school. Without one you didn't seem to count. She wondered, though, if giving in to the guy most of the time to keep peace was fair. Why shouldn't he compromise, too—fifty-fifty?

The tables were filling with diners. Her mouth watered at the aroma of tomatoes and cheese baking. It was noisy with conversation, kids playing video games, and a TV screen showing Disney cartoons.

Cliff waved to her from across the room where he was getting a pitcher of cola, and glasses to bring to them. He motioned for her to pick up the pizza.

"Cliff needs help. Be right back." Alex slipped out of her chair and made her way between tables to Cliff.

"The pizza receipt's in my pocket," he said. "You'll have to get it; my hands are full."

She slowly drew the paper from his shirt pocket, a surge of pleasure jolting through her, making her legs weak. Just that brief touch, that small connection in the middle of the crowded room, was all it took.

"Better get the pizza," Cliff said softly, watching her.

"Yes." She moved to the counter in a kind of trance, handed over the receipt, and carried the fragrant, steaming pizza back to the table, eyes on Cliff. It wasn't until she placed it in front of everyone that she noticed. It was laden with pepperoni, green peppers, sausage, mushrooms, olives and anchovies—except for one section covered only with cheese and vegetables.

He had remembered her mother's preference.

After pizza they drove to the small playground near her house. "Race you!" Cliff called as soon as he parked. He took off across the grass for the swings, looking back and laughing as Alex cried, "No fair! No fair!" because he hadn't warned her. She sprinted after him, loving the chance to be outdoors on such a mild summer evening.

He reached the swings first, dropped onto a canvas seat, and began pumping. Alex arrived a moment later, face flushed, hair wild, drew the next swing close to her hips, backed off as far as she could, then hopped onto the seat. In a moment she was swinging almost as high as Cliff.

It was a perfect time of evening—cool and still with enough light to see the joggers circling the park and the two boys skating the obstacle course they'd set up on the basketball court. For a while they swung together contentedly, without speaking.

"Dad's driving me crazy," Cliff said, breaking the silence. "Can you imagine? I've been accepted by UC. The deposit's in for housing and everything, and he's still arguing that I shouldn't go, that I'm wasting his money if I don't know what I want to do. He keeps bringing up that sports scholarship I turned down because I didn't want to go to a third-rate school."

"Did you tell him he ought to be *proud* UC accepted you?"

Cliff threw her a grateful look. "Shouldn't he know without my saying?" He jumped off the swing. Head down, he trudged through the sand to the cement walk, bent suddenly, and plucked a stone from the ground. With all his might he threw it at a nearby garbage can. The clatter as the can toppled rang out in the still night. "Damn!" he exclaimed, punching his fist into his hand. "It's a war zone at home!"

Alex dragged her feet, slowing the swing. "Your parents seemed so nice, at graduation...." Even as she spoke the words she realized they weren't true. She recalled how Mr. Vandermeer treated Diane, the strange way she felt when he looked at *her*, the way Mrs. Vandermeer hardly said a word.

"They're good at putting on a show in public. You should see them at home. Screaming at each other. Arguing over money, over Diane, over Dad's drinking, over everything. Sometimes—at night—I hear..." He didn't finish the sentence. "And Di... Oh, I don't know. I shouldn't be talking like this."

"Why?" Alex slid off the swing and went to Cliff. She threw her arms around his waist and leaned her head against his back. "If you can't talk to me, who can you talk to?"

Cliff pulled her hands tighter around him and leaned back against her. She could feel his body relaxing under her touch.

"I don't know what I'd do without you, Alex. You're the first girl I've known who really understands and accepts me—warts and all."

"Warts? You have no warts! You're perfect!" she teased. These were the best times, when he admitted how much he needed her, when he showed his vulnerability. When she felt she could help him. This was what love was all about.

"You're the best thing that ever happened to me, too," she echoed. "And I'll always be here for you, no matter what."

EIGHT

When she arrived at the
Y with Cliff the next morning, some of the early comers
were already on swings, playing basketball and hand-
ball, or just standing around, not quite awake. Mothers
or fathers were arriving with children, bringing them to
a table across the field to be signed in. Some immediately ran off to play while others hung back, not ready to
leave their parent.

"See you later, Cone," Cliff said, blowing a kiss. He
crossed the field to where the older kids played. Alex
found Karen and helped line up the little children for a
game of kickball.

"Get home all right?" Karen asked, as if she could
hardly wait to ask. "Cliff come back for you?"

She bent to tie a child's shoelace, averting her face.
"There was a misunderstanding. We got together later."
She gave the little girl a hug, then sent her off to play.

"With Cliff that happens, a *lot*. When we were going
together—"

"I know all about that!" Alex said, cutting her short. "And it's not the same! There's Justin. Looks like he doesn't want to stay. I'll see if I can help." She jogged off, glad to end the discussion.

Justin's mother, dressed in a business suit, appeared to be pushing her son toward the sign-in table. His little legs propelled twice as fast as his mother's. As Alex drew closer she saw that his eyes were red and puffy. She felt an overwhelming tenderness for him.

"Come on, sweetie. Don't fuss!" his mother was saying, "*Everyone* loves summer camp!"

When they were nearly at the table, Justin put on the brakes. "I don't wanna!"

"Don't be a baby!" His mother bent to stare him straight in the eye. "Come on now. You'll have a great time and I'll see you tonight. I have to go now. Come on, honey! Let's see a smile." She plucked her son's hand off her arm and looked like she didn't know what to do next, when Alex arrived.

"Hi, Justin! Remember me?" Alex squatted to eye level. "Guess what I've got? A *surprise* for you!" She held one hand behind her back. "Bet you can't guess what it is!"

Justin plugged a thumb in his mouth, threw one anxious glance in his mother's direction, and focused on Alex.

"He's so terribly shy and fearful of change," his mother confided. "I just hate leaving him like this, but

I'm late." She checked her watch. "I really *must* go."

"He'll be fine." Alex smiled at Justin. "Look, honey, look what I have for you!" She brought her fist forward and slowly opened it. "See? Know what they are?"

Justin shook his head and moved closer.

"Beans. *Magic* beans, like in Jack and the Beanstalk." She stood. "Let's go put them in water fast so they'll root or they'll lose their magic! Say bye-bye to Mommy!"

"Bye, sweetie," his mother said, but Justin didn't answer. With hardly a glance back he took Alex's hand and went with her.

"You hold them." Alex opened Justin's fist and slid the beans onto his palm. "In a few days they'll sprout, then guess who'll plant them?"

Justin gazed up at her, eyes bright and hopeful.

"You!" She put an arm around his shoulder. "Then, you'll have to come each day to take care of them and watch them grow. Okay?"

Justin nodded, eyes intent on the three beans in the hand stretched out in front of him.

Alex glanced around, wondering if Cliff had seen how she handled Justin, but he was down in the lower playing field with the older kids. As she came back to the sign-in table Brian winked approval and pretended to applaud. She felt heat rise to her face.

Right after lunch the buses arrived for an outing to the roller rink. The playground soon swarmed with noisy Y campers bubbling with energy.

Brian took charge, calling off groups for different buses. Alex followed Karen onto the bus with the K-3s and helped settle them just as Cliff's kids climbed on.

"Maybe we can sit together later," he said, stopping in the aisle beside her seat for an instant.

"I'll save a seat." She moved to the window, leaving a sweater on the seat beside her.

"This taken?" Karen asked a moment later.

"I'm saving it for Cliff."

"Oh." Karen settled down across the aisle and leaned over to chat.

The noise level rose to bedlam with shouting and screaming and visiting back and forth when Brian climbed onto the bus. "All right, everyone! Listen up! This bus doesn't move until everyone sits with backs against the seat, feet on the floor. No fighting, no changing seats, got that? All *right!* Who's going to have a great time?"

"*We* are!" Alex and the children screamed.

"And who are *we?*"

"Y campers!"

"Give us the 'Y'…" He held a hand to his ear.

The bus erupted into loud, enthusiastic song.

Brian grinned. "Then, let's *go!*"

The bus rumbled out of the parking lot to the street and headed on down the road to the freeway.

Brian swung down the aisle, eyeing the empty seat. "This yours?" He held up the sweater.

"Yes, but I'm saving the seat."

"For me?" He dropped the sweater on her lap and before she could answer, sat down.

"These outings are fun for the kids but hard work for us. Someone almost always throws up. Gas fumes, the rocking and turning, the excitement and all."

She smiled stiffly, feeling trapped.

"You're doing a good job with Justin, Alex. I've been watching," he said.

Alex clasped her hands tightly, wondering if Cliff saw, worrying what he might think.

"That business of having Justin plant the beans gives him an incentive to come each day. That was inventive."

"Thanks."

"He'll be okay. Lots of kids are scared the first day or so. They get over it."

"His mother said he's very shy and hates change. I wish I could help. He's a sweet kid." She glanced anxiously behind her but couldn't spot Cliff.

"Draw him out," Brian suggested. "Use your story-telling talent. You see, I've read your file."

"Thanks," Alex said again and turned silent.

"What do you think?" Brian asked.

She shrugged. "I don't know. Maybe. I could try."

"Good. Oh, the noise!" Brian jumped up and faced the back. "Listen up, guys! Cool it!" He covered his ears and grimaced. "I can't hear myself think! I can't hear Alexandra and she's sitting right next to me, so bring the volume down! Way down!" He dropped back into his seat.

Alex cringed. Now Cliff knew for sure Brian was beside her and she'd done nothing to encourage him.

"Talk about being shy," Brian said. "*You* don't say much. Tell me. You like roller skating? Any good at it?"

"I'm okay."

"Don't listen to her," Karen said across the aisle. "She's modest. I've seen her with Cliff. She's *good*!"

Alex leaned around Brian to speak. "Cliff's a terrific skater. He makes anyone look good."

"I'm a real klutz on wheels," Brian confided. "Maybe you can show me a few things."

That's all she needed! Alex turned to the window, hoping to discourage him. She wanted Cliff to see she was making every effort not to be friendly.

Karen took over the conversation until the buses pulled into the skating rink lot. They parked and the doors swung open. "Line up! Stay with your group! No pushing!" Karen shouted, leading the way down the steps.

"Let's go!" Alex called. "Everyone out! Adam!" She leveled a warning gaze at a second-grader pulling a little girl's hair. The boy grinned and moved back. Soon everyone was out into the hot, smoggy day, lining up behind their counselors, and marching up the ramp past the ticket counter to the air-conditioned skating rink.

For the next half hour Alex kept busy outfitting her

children in the right size skates and helping put them on. But even as she smiled and joked and helped first-time skaters to their wobbly feet she was conscious of Cliff. He'd skated right past without saying a word.

The place smelled musty of dust and feet, and it throbbed with the loud, pounding organ music and the squeals and shrieks of small children. Anxious to be out on the floor where she could judge Cliff's mood the moment their eyes met, she hurried the last child into skates and sent him on his way. Then she skated along the rug to the rink floor.

"Oh, Justin!" The boy clung to the guardrail separating the viewing area from the skaters. Trying to stay upright, he bent back and forth like a weed in the wind. "Here, give me your hands!" Skating backward, she pulled him along. His face reflected joy and terror as he rolled forward, bent at the waist, legs far apart. But he learned quickly and soon she was able to send him off on his own.

Alex skated around and around, helping a fallen child, taking another for a quick circle of the rink, or gliding along on her own, but always conscious of Cliff. Sometimes he'd roll by, leading a pack of older kids, or she'd see him leave to get a drink. And then, suddenly, he skated up to her and synchronized his speed to hers. "Remember last time we were here?" He put an arm around her waist. "Let's show these guys what we can do."

He *wasn't* angry! Her heart turned over. His touch, his familiar scent made her dizzy. She picked up his rhythm and soon they were stroking hard, speeding around the rink in perfect harmony. In a blur she glimpsed Brian leaning on the guardrail in the viewing area, watching. Counselors swept children off the rink floor or herded them against the walls to give them room. Cliff led her through all the intricate steps and movements they had practiced together and they were good. She knew it, could sense it in the hush around her. She felt exultant, as if she'd never skated better in her life.

"We deserved it," Cliff whispered when the music stopped and the applause began. He hugged her for an instant, then children swarmed onto the floor and crowded them. "Teach me how to spin like that, oh, please, please! Teach me what you did!"

Alex skated away. She needed a drink, a dark place to hide until her pulse returned to normal. Children intercepted her, asking questions, sharing small achievements, wanting to know how much longer they could stay. She pushed her long hair back from her damp forehead and bent over the water fountain.

"That was some performance," Brian said, skating to her side, "for a girl who's 'just an okay' skater!"

She straightened and brushed the water from her lips. Instinctively, she glanced toward the rink to see where Cliff was.

"Where'd you learn to skate like that?"

"Took lessons when I was little. Thought I wanted to be a professional."

"And?"

"And it takes five hours of practice a day and a huge commitment from family. And, well... I guess I didn't want it enough."

"Storyteller, roller skater, psychologist. Pretty woman," Brian counted on his fingers, smiling. "What else are you?"

Pretty? She covered her nose.

"Like a soda?" Brian turned to the vending machine and deposited three quarters before she could answer. "Diet or regular?"

"Nothing, thanks. I really have to get back to the kids."

"Wait!" Brian skated to her side. "Look—I don't understand. Every time I try to talk, you turn away or walk away—or *skate* away. Like now." He put a restraining hand on her arm. "I'm not a monster, Alex, and I figured you and Cliff are going together. I'm just trying to get to know you better. I do that with every new counselor. Are you afraid of me? Do you dislike me for some reason?"

"No. No! Of course not!" Brian wasn't trying to come on to her, as Cliff thought. She felt like an idiot, the way she'd behaved.

"Can we be friends?"

"We *are* friends."

He held out a hand.

She hesitated, then took it. His grip was firm and he released her quickly.

"Go once around the rink with a skating klutz like me?"

"I saw you on the floor with Karen and Stefanie. You weren't bad."

"Not so *good*, either. So?"

She almost laughed at his look of innocent, boyish hope.

"Sure." It would be unfriendly to refuse him and surely Cliff would understand when she explained.

"Let's go!" She skated on ahead. "But only *once* around."

She was kneeling on the floor trying to untie a knot in one of the children's shoe skates when Cliff stopped behind her. "We have to talk."

She glanced up, alarmed by the frigid tone of voice. "Now?" She scurried to her feet as if caught doing something wrong.

"Later." Cliff rolled away leaving her looking after him. Her stomach lurched as she bent again to undo the knot.

When she climbed on the bus she hurried to the seat beside Karen to avoid Brian and sat with hands squeezed between her knees. What was it now? Was it because she skated with Brian? But it was so innocent! How could she have refused? She never seemed able to please Cliff anymore, no matter how hard she tried. She'd given up friends, dressed as he wanted, gave him time taken away from her family, avoided even talking to other boys—but it wasn't enough. And lately his patience was wearing thin.

"Something wrong?" Karen asked as the bus filled. Subdued by the afternoon's activity, most of the campers leaned their heads against a window or talked softly.

"Just tired."

Cliff led his group onto the bus. *Look at me; show me a sign it's okay with us,* she willed, devouring him with her eyes, but he passed without a nod. It felt like a knife had been turned in her stomach.

"I'm tired, too." Karen stretched and yawned. "These days when I get home I can hardly keep my eyes open during dinner."

Only half listening, Alex stared out the window. The bus moved slowly from the parking lot. Railroad tracks paralleled the road with industrial buildings beside the tracks. A dirty haze blurred the sky. She felt the way the sky looked, heavy and dismal.

"What's eating Cliff?" Karen asked.

Adrenaline rushed to Alex's head. "What do you mean?"

"He's got that—that *sour* look, like he's fuming about something. I know it well; boy, do I know it! What is it this time?"

Alex bristled. There she went again, trying to put Cliff down and undermine their relationship. What was it with Karen? She noticed everything Cliff said and did.

"You and Cliff have been going together—what is it—six, seven months?"

"Five. Why?"

"He's complicated, isn't he?"

"What's wrong with that?"

"Don't be angry, Alex. I'm just trying to be a friend. What I mean is, Cliff shows one face to the world and another when you get to know him. I guess he told you—we went together for almost a year before we broke up."

"I know."

"Did he say *why* we broke up?"

"Sure!" Karen went "women's libber" on him, insisting on having her way on every little thing. He didn't like aggressive, unfeminine women, he'd said.

"I bet he didn't tell you the *whole* story."

"Oh?"

"No, he wouldn't. It would make him look bad. Did he say I wouldn't let him get away with pushing me around? Does he get rough with you?"

"Of course not!"

"Maybe you haven't known him long enough, but you'll find out." Karen twisted a thread on her jeans, silent for a long moment. "I seemed to bring out the worst in him. Sometimes he got so *angry*!" She chewed at a thumbnail, searching Alex's eyes. "He'd... well..." She didn't finish the sentence. "He's terrific in lots of ways and I was crazy about him, but no guy's gonna treat *me* like that!"

Alex stared at Karen, hoping she'd go on.

"Maybe he changed, but I doubt it. You're pretty young for him. He can probably boss you easier and you'd put up with it. Not me. I'm not the kind who'll put up with *any*thing." She chuckled humorlessly. "I'm not the submissive type. Are you?"

"Of course not!" Alex answered in a huff.

Karen swung around suddenly and said, "Joannie, please stop kicking my seat! I mean it!" When she turned back she was almost apologetic. "Forget it. I'm sorry I said anything. It was probably just *me*."

The bus lumbered onto the freeway and Alex leaned a cheek against the window, looking at without seeing the passing office towers against the backdrop of smoggy mountains. What did Karen mean about bringing out the worst in Cliff? Lately, it seemed that's what she did, too. *Was* she submissive?

She wondered if guys thought about relationships as much as girls did. Girls had to be so careful, make so many concessions and compromises. Was that what *submissive* meant? Still, it was worth it to keep Cliff loving her. As Karen said, he was terrific in *lots* of ways. She vowed to be more understanding. Surely whatever it was Cliff wanted to talk about, they could deal with.

But later, as she busied herself hanging some of the day's artwork, she felt a growing sense of doom. Almost everyone had gone home already. Only one counselor and the children in late day care remained— yet Cliff hadn't come to her. Last time she'd seen him he'd left the building with three children in tow. She worriedly nibbled her thumbnail. Had he gone home without her again? She crossed the room to the window facing the parking lot and the fear eased. His car was still there.

"Ready?" Cliff asked a few minutes later, coming up behind her.

"Oh!" The blood rushed to her face and her heart jumped with relief. "Where were you? I worried. I thought maybe..." She stopped herself, babbling, afraid to sound accusing. "Just a sec, I'll get my things." She ran to the closet, threw her jacket around her shoulders, and hurried back to him. "Ready!" She smiled, conscious of a growing panic when he didn't respond.

"Bye!" she called with false gaiety to the counselor left with the late pick-up kids. "See you tomorrow!"

"Bye, Alex... Cliff..."

Cliff reached around her and opened the door, then guided her across the playing field, a firm hand on her back. He was furious. She could feel it in his silence, in the pressure on her back. Maybe, if she started the conversation, if she explained before he got started, it would be okay.

"I know you're upset about something, and maybe it's about Brian talking to me and me skating with him, but I want to explain. I really tried..."

They had reached the car and he cut her short. "Get

in the car, Alex. I don't want to hear your excuses. Just get in the car."

"But Cliff, please. Listen to me. I..." One look at his face and she knew it was useless. She opened the car door and climbed in, folded her hands, and waited for Cliff to get in beside her.

"Now," he said, as soon as he was seated. "Now you can explain." He gripped the steering wheel and stared straight ahead.

She turned so she could watch him and the words tumbled out. "I said I'd save you a seat on the bus to the rink, and I did. But then Brian came and saw the empty place and he sat down before I could stop him. That's all there was to it!"

"You couldn't say, 'I'm saving this seat for Cliff'?" His lips twisted.

"I did! I said, 'I'm saving this seat,' and he said, 'For me!' Honestly, Cliff, what could I do? I mean—Brian's in charge. How could I say, 'Don't sit here'?"

He swung around, grabbed her by the arms and shook her. "Don't try to con *me*! You could have said anything you wanted. I never realized it before, but you're a little flirt. I saw you making up to him—all smiles! I saw!" His grip tightened and he shook her harder. "I *told* you to stay away from him! Why don't you listen?"

"Cliff, stop!" she cried. "You're hurting me!"

"What about how you hurt me? Know how I felt

when you deserted me on the rink floor and went off to Brian?"

"I didn't! I didn't leave you to see Brian. I was thirsty, that's why I left. Let go! Please!"

"You weren't thirsty! You wanted to get off the floor so Brian could come after you! You tried *real* hard to stay away, all right! Skating with him! Showing off *holding hands!* His arm around your waist! Geez! I see red just *thinking* about it!"

"He asked me to! I had to! It was only for one song!" Would anything she say convince him? She was crying now.

"He *asked* you to! And if he asked you to kiss him, you'd do that, too?" Cliff dug his fingers deeper into her arms. "How could I have been so wrong about you? If you act like that right in front of me, what are you like when we're *not* together? You're a tease, a rotten tease!" Suddenly, he let go of her arms and slapped her.

"Cliff!" Alex cried. She touched her cheek and burst into tears.

Cliff's face turned white, then red. "What have I done? Oh, Alex, I'm sorry! I'm so sorry!" He reached out awkwardly, trying to raise her chin so she'd look at him. He stroked her hair, kissed her hands, her nose, her lips, tried to draw her rigid body close. "Please, Alex. I'm sorry! I didn't mean it! I'm sorry!"

She rubbed her bruised arms and couldn't look at him.

"Please, Cone, forgive me. You know I'd never hurt you! I don't know what got into me!" He stared at her with concern. "I just got so angry! You promised to stay away from Brian and when I saw you two together, I just went crazy! Can you understand? I can't bear you being with anyone else! How can I make it up to you? I know you'd never go for that nerd. Please, Cone, please—forgive me!"

So, this was what Karen meant. When Cliff got mad enough, he got physical. She felt empty, unsure what to say, how to feel. All she wanted was to go home. She wiped her eyes with the back of a hand. Cliff pulled a tissue from a box and gently patted her cheek. "I swear," he whispered hoarsely. "I'll never, *never* do that again. I swear! Are you all right?"

She nodded but couldn't give him a reassuring smile. "I'm all right, it's okay, but let's go home now, okay?"

"Sure!" He let out a deep, mournful sigh and started the car. "You're an angel. I don't know what I'd do if you didn't forgive me!"

When she reached home she went directly to her room, locked the door, and hurried to the big mirror over her dresser. She touched the cheek Cliff had slapped. It was still sore, slightly swollen, but the redness had faded so it looked almost normal. She examined her upper arms and worriedly chewed her lip.

There were red marks where Cliff's fingers had pressed. She touched them and winced. Maybe, if she applied cold water, if she rubbed them, they wouldn't show.

"Alex? You in there?" Kim rattled the doorknob. "Why's the door locked?"

"Stay out! Go away! I'm busy!" she screamed.

"I need to talk to you about that boy at school! Please, Alex! Let me in!"

"Later! Go away!" Frantic, her eyes searched the room for a way to hide her bruises. She ran to the closet, yanking off her T-shirt as she went.

"I'm coming in!"

"No!" The clothes rod was a tight jumble of blouses, sweaters, and jackets. She grabbed the first long-sleeved shirt she found and hurriedly drew it on.

"Told you! Here I am!" Kim pranced to a stop in front of the closet. "Bet you forgot I could get in through the bathroom!" she announced with a jubilant grin.

Alex slammed the closet door and dropped down on her bed, buttoning the sleeves. "All right, pest. You've got five minutes. What about the boy?"

Her sister wore a T-shirt and shorts. She bounced onto the opposite end of the bed and crossed her long, bare legs. She studied Alex, head cocked. "You sick?"

"No!"

"How come you're wearing that heavy shirt? It's hot!"

"Well, I'm cold!" Alex glared at Kim, hugging herself as if she really was cold. Did Kim notice the swelling on her cheek? "Okay, kiddo," she said, eager to divert her sister's attention. "Better start talking. What's this about a boy? You've used up one minute already. I'll give you four more and then—out!"

**on't you be hot in that** long-sleeved shirt?" Alex's mother asked the next morning. "It's going to be close to a hundred today."

"The Y's air-conditioned. Sometimes it gets cold," she said, taking her dishes to the sink so her mother wouldn't see her face. The bruises looked even worse today, dark blue-black with imprints of fingers. How long would it take for them to fade so she could wear summer tops again? She busied herself fixing a sandwich lunch, half listening to Kim and her mother's chatter.

Every time she let herself remember Cliff's rage— how he screamed at her and squeezed her arms and slapped her—a lump grew in her throat. He shouldn't have done it. She hadn't flirted, but even if she had, he shouldn't have done it.

Cliff wasn't abusive; look how he protected his sister. If he'd been rough with Karen, it was out of frustration. She always challenged him, was too demanding, pushed him too far. *She* wasn't like that. If Cliff blew up, it came from fear of losing her; it came from love. She felt a certain pride in knowing he cared so much he lost control. She'd heard girls tell how boyfriends slapped them sometimes and it only proved how much they were loved.

She shook her head, trying to clear the confusion, leaned both hands on the counter, and blinked back tears. Her father never hit *her* mother. The only time Alex had ever been spanked was when she'd run into the street and nearly been run over—but that was years ago. Did a guy *ever* have the right to hit his girl? She had to stop going over what happened, forgive, and try harder to please Cliff.

"I'll get it!" Kim called when the bell rang, jumping up and running to the door. That would be *him*! Alex's heart thudded. He'd expect she'd rush to him like nothing happened and she felt like running back to her room to hide under the covers.

"That child!" Mrs. Cummings joined Alex at the kitchen sink. "She's just crazy about your young man! And why not? Look how he treats you. So respectful! None of this honking a horn and expecting you to come running."

Alex gripped the sink edge, ears keyed to Cliff's voice and approaching footsteps. When he phoned last night she'd been brief, said she was tired, hung up quickly.

"Look what he brought!" Kim danced into the kitchen.

"Sssh!" Cliff, just behind Kim, raised a finger to his lips and hid a hand behind his back. "Hi, Mrs. Cummings! Hi, Cone!"

Alex turned and forced a smile. He wore a new blue polo and white shorts. His dark hair fell over one eye. He held out a bouquet of red and white roses.

"Oh, they're just beautiful!" Mrs. Cummings exclaimed.

"Oooh! You're so lucky!" Kim said.

Alex took the flowers, closed her eyes, and inhaled the sweet scent. "They *are* beautiful! Thanks, Cliff!" He looked so uneasy and repentant, she felt guilty at not showing more enthusiasm.

"What's the occasion, Cliff?" Mrs. Cummings asked.

"Nothing special. Cone deserves it." Cliff rolled his eyes heavenward. "Oh, man!"

"Thanks," Alex said again. She laid the bouquet on the kitchen counter and reached for her day pack. "Mom, please put these in water, would you? We have to go." She pecked Cliff quickly on the cheek then hurried to the front door.

"I'm really sorry about last night, Alex. I didn't hurt you, did I?" Cliff asked when the door closed behind them.

Alex touched her bruised arm. "It's nothing. It'll go away."

"But you're still angry, aren't you?"

"Not really," she answered quickly.

"Then how about a hug? I need a big one, and a kiss—*something* to show I'm forgiven!" He cocked his head in his usual teasing way.

"How's this?" She gave him a quick hug and kiss, then pulled away and got into the car. Cliff ran around to the driver's side and climbed in beside her. "You can do better than that. Come here." He pulled her close and kissed her tenderly. His familiar scent, his touch and kisses made everything seem normal again. And then she noticed the time. "Oh, Cliff! It's late! Brian will be furious!"

"*Brian! Brian!* There you go again!"

Alex stiffened. "But we're supposed to... I didn't mean anything. It's just that—"

Cliff opened his mouth, then shut it. "You're right, I just see red every time you say his name." He touched her lips, swung around, and started the car. "It's going to be better, I promise, Cone." He reached for her hand and pressed it to his cheek.

The Y pool was steamy and smelled of chlorine. It echoed with voices and splashing. The big kids were jumping off the diving board, the younger ones paddling across the pool, and the littlest ones—those Alex worked with—playing in the shallow end.

Karen had asked about her bruises when they changed into swimsuits earlier.

"Oh, that? I bumped into the edge of a door last night. Clumsy me," Alex had answered, drawing on her long-sleeved shirt.

"*Both* arms?"

She felt a flush creep over her face as she slammed the locker shut.

"It wasn't Cliff getting a little rough?" Karen threw a towel over her shoulder.

Alex stood straighter. "You know what Cliff did this morning? He brought me a gorgeous bouquet of roses when he came to pick me up!"

"He does that. I used to get daffodils."

"He does *what*?" Alex challenged, her heart thudding so hard it filled her ears. "Does *what*?"

"I think you know." Impatient faces peered around the lockers at them. "Let's go swimmers! Let's go!" Karen jogged away, blowing a whistle. Fuming, Alex followed.

Now, in the shallow end of the pool, with six of the nonswimming kids clustered around her, Alex put the conversation out of her head. In the deep end Cliff was calling to some boys jumping off the diving board, his voice echoing off the walls. Across the pool Brian talked with a counselor, but his eyes swept the room. *Don't look at me, please,* she begged silently as she turned to her shivering kids to start their first swim lesson.

"Once," she began, in a storytelling voice, "there was a beautiful dolphin princess who lost her way in the big sea. She was terribly scared. More than anything, she wanted to get back to her friends."

Justin, who had been standing at the edge of the group, pressed in closer. She went on with the story, but part of her brain was operating elsewhere, thinking about Justin. He was a quiet, introspective child who loved to be read to, loved to hear stories. Maybe Brian was right. She could help him through storytelling!

"Do you know how she let her friends know where to find her?" she went on. "Christopher?"

"She made loud noises?"

"She rode on the back of a whale!" Brendan called out.

"Anyone else?"

"She waited till her mommy came?"

"Uh-huh."

Justin's hand flew up.

"Yes?"

"She—rang a bell?"

"You all had good answers and you're all nearly right. The dolphin princess blew *bubbles*. Like this." Alex took a deep breath, closed her eyes, and lowered her face into the water. She blew loud bubbles until all the air had left her lungs. Then she straightened up, squeezed her wet hair back from her face with both hands, and opened her eyes. "That's what she did. The bubbles made sounds that went through all the ocean to her friends and that's how they found her. Now—let's do what I just did, what the dolphin princess did."

Fifteen minutes later she had each child bubbling water like little blowfish. Even Justin. She felt elated. In another few days she hoped they'd all be doing dead-man floats.

"Nice going. You'll have them swimming like porpoises before the summer's over," Brian said, as she led the children back to the locker room.

"Hope so." He eyed her wet shirt, and for a moment she feared he'd ask why she went into the pool wearing it. "Let's go, guys!" she called out, hurrying the children along and drawing her shirt closer. She flashed Brian a quick smile and glanced behind her. All she needed was for Cliff to see her talking with Brian again.

ELEVEN

"Alex, can you stay a bit?" Brian asked two weeks later as she got ready to leave. "I wouldn't ask, except Justin's mother is running late and he'd feel a lot more secure if you're here. How about it?"

For an instant she thought about Cliff waiting, but it probably wouldn't be for long and he understood how she felt about Justin. She'd had a little time alone with the boy, enough to gain his confidence. Once she even helped him summarize a story before the group. Perhaps now she could lead him further in storytelling.

"Sure," she said. "I just have to tell Cliff. We ride together."

"I noticed." Brian smiled.

Cliff had been wonderful these last few weeks, more thoughtful and loving than he'd ever been. After work they'd drive to the lake, sit in the car, and talk, or walk hand in hand along the shore. Sometimes she'd bring marshmallows to toss to the fish, laughing as they swarmed up from the murky depths, fighting to get at the treats. He'd sent her love notes, bought her a bracelet with a heart charm, told her again and again how much she meant to him. What had happened that day faded in her memory as the bruises had.

"If there's a problem about getting home later, I can take you," Brian said.

"Oh, thanks, but I'll get home okay!" She'd walk if Cliff couldn't come back for her. She'd call her mother. But one thing she'd never do is give Cliff reason to worry if she rode with Brian.

With most of the children gone, the activity room seemed too quiet and even a little sad. Only a half dozen children remained, playing with games or puzzles, gazing out the windows wistfully. She found a picture book they could all enjoy and gathered them around. Sitting on a low stool with the children on the floor, she read "Ig Lives in a Cave," about a prehistoric boy and his family.

"This is the chapter in which Ig wants to give his mother something special for her birthday," she said.

Justin's hand went up. "Tomorrow's *my* mommy's birthday!" he called.

"That's nice. Now sit down and listen." Alex read how Ig tried to paint a picture for his mother, but failed, how he tried to carve a club, but failed. "'Mother,' Ig said on her birthday. 'I did not make you a present. I do not know how to make anything. I am sorry.'" Alex glanced up at the eager, listening faces. "'Ig,' his mother replied, 'you do know how to make something. And you know how to make it better than anyone. You make it with your arms. Can you guess what it is?'"

Alex put the book down and asked, "Can anyone guess what Ig could make better than anyone?"

Justin leaned forward, eyes glistening. No one answered.

"It was a *hug*!" Alex said. "He made a big warm hug with his arms. Like this! That was his birthday present to Mother!"

Justin waved his hand anxiously. "Tomorrow's *my* mommy's birthday!" he repeated.

"I know, Justin. Do *you* have a present for her?"

Justin shook his head, a furrow of anxiety between his eyes.

"Then we'll do something about that!" she said.

One by one the other children left as parents arrived. Finally, only Justin remained. Brian slipped into the room to report that Justin's mother was stuck in traffic. Could Alex stay a while longer?

"We'll be fine," Alex said, taking Justin's hand and leading him to a table. "We're going to make Justin's mom a beautiful birthday card. And then I'm going to show him how to make a *very* special gift."

"A hug, like Ig did?" Justin asked.

"Even better!"

"Good," Brian said as he left. "I'll be in the office if you need me."

Alex brought out paper, scissors, and crayons. She found a package of lacy paper doilies and cut one into a heart, and Justin pasted it sloppily onto a sheet of red paper. With a red marker pen Alex wrote across the heart "Happy Birthday, Mommy." Below, Justin laboriously printed, "Love, Justin."

"There!" Alex said, triumphantly. She folded a sheet of paper and stapled it into an envelope for the card. "Your mother will love it!" Justin smiled up at her happily.

"And now we'll work on that *special* treat."

For the next fifteen minutes Alex reread the Ig chapter until Justin knew it by heart. She felt a certain urgency, worried that Justin's mother would arrive before they were ready. After the third rereading she said, "Now, *you* tell it." She sat back with arms crossed and a smile on her face. "Stand up and let me see you pretend to be Ig. Show me everything he felt and tell me everything he said."

Justin jumped up, eager, forgetting his shyness. He remembered the story almost perfectly and even imitated Ig trying to paint or carve. Finally, the climax of the story came. In the saddest little voice he said, "Mother. I did not make you a present. I do not know how to make *anything*. I am sorry." He pretended to wipe away a tear. "And then Ig's mama said, 'Ig, you do know how to make something. You make it better than anyone.'"

"Oh, Justin!" Alex cried, delighted. "Oh, sweetie! Come here and show me!"

Without a pause, Justin went straight into Alex's arms. She pressed his small body close as he gave her a warm, loving hug. "Sweetie," she said. "Your mommy is going to be thrilled, and you're going to be a wonderful storyteller!"

"She's here," Brian said, putting his head around the door. "Justin's mother."

Alex swallowed the lump in her throat and took Justin by the hand. "Tonight," she whispered, "just before bedtime, you give your mommy the card you made. And then you tell her the Ig story as you told me. And don't forget that hug!"

She glanced at her watch and a surge of electricity swept down her arms. It was so *late*! She'd told Cliff she surely wouldn't be longer than half an hour and here it was over an hour!

"Thank you so much!" Justin's mother gushed. "I had no choice! My meeting ran late and then I ran into awful traffic and…"

Alex fidgeted through the thanks and apologies, her mind on Cliff. Now, it would be too late to go to the lake. Would Cliff still be waiting? She should go straight home but then he'd be annoyed.

As soon as Justin and his mother left, she grabbed her day pack and rushed out to the landing above the parking lot. With a sigh of relief she saw Cliff's red Mustang below.

"Got a ride?" Brian asked, coming out the door behind her.

"Cliff's waiting!" *Stay away from me*, she silently begged as she skipped down the steps to the lot, but Brian stayed beside her, talking about the trip to Disneyland the next week.

"There's Cliff!" she said. He was leaning on the trunk of his car watching. "Bye!" She flew down the last steps and ran across the parking lot before Brian could say more.

"Hi! Sorry I'm late!" Her heart beat fast and then nearly stopped at the look on his face.

"You hanging around Brian *again*?" Cliff asked, a cold edge to his voice. "Is that why you stayed late? You keep me waiting an hour and a half while you're playing around with *him*? I ought to let you *walk* home!" His voice rose with each sentence and for a second she thought he might hit her.

"It wasn't that way at all!" Alex protested. "I told you! Justin's mother got here late. Didn't you see her? I was with Justin all this time, not Brian!"

"*Sure*! Like when you walked out with him! Why didn't *he* stay with Justin, if he was going to hang around anyway till all the kids' parents came?"

"I don't know! Maybe he had things to do. Maybe he thought I'd be better at—"

"Cut the crap! He stayed to be with *you*, that's why! And you encourage him! Get in the car!" He grabbed her arm.

"Stop it, Cliff! You're wrong! He's not after me! I'm not after him! You've no reason to be jealous!"

"Me, jealous? Ho ho ho! Don't give yourself so much credit, kid! Why should I be jealous when I could have any girl in school! Just look at you—that nose, that—hair!"

Her hand flew to her face and hair, and she wanted to die. In a moment of closeness she'd confided how she felt about her looks and now he was using it to hurt her!

"Get in the car! You heard me! What are you waiting for?" He gave her a push.

"Oh!" She struck her knee on the edge of the door, winced, but hurriedly did as she was told. Now she knew what Cliff really thought of her. It hurt more than the physical pain. Now he'd drop her, as he had dropped Karen, and find someone else. All because of Brian. Damn Brian! It was all his fault!

"Cliff, listen please!" she begged, near tears.

"Shut *up*!" He climbed into the driver's seat.

"Brian wasn't even in the room with me until Justin's mother came!"

"You're defending him again! I told you to shut up!" He glared at her and squeezed her thigh.

"Don't!" She tried to pry his hand off.

"You're *nothing* without me!"

"Don't!" she whispered. "Cliff, stop it!" Tears started down her cheek. She swiped impatiently at them. "You promised."

"*Cry*! Go ahead, *cry*. That's all you're good for!" He started the car and screeched out of the parking lot.

"Where are you going?" she asked when he didn't go toward home.

"Where we would have gone if you'd told *Brian* you couldn't stick around!"

"It's late!"

"'It's late!'" he imitated. "Whose fault is that?"

She was expected home by six thirty. If they went to the lake, they'd be gone until eight. Her parents would worry. He knew that. "I should phone..." she whispered.

"'I should phone!'" he repeated.

"Why are you *doing* this?"

"Don't you get it?" he said in a voice heavy with fury. "I trusted you, opened up to you, shared all my secrets, and what do you do? Betray me! Why? Why? Why?"

"I didn't do *anything!*" she cried in exasperation. "It's all your imagination!" She clamped her mouth shut. This wasn't how to deal with Cliff. He was trying to apologize, to show how hurt he felt. If she kept defending herself Cliff would only get angrier. He never meant to harm her; she had to hold on to that belief. He couldn't help how he behaved; he learned it from his father. It was up to her to be understanding and tender, to teach him that he didn't have to act that way with her.

Best to humor him, let him get that rage and fear

out. It was up to the woman to keep the peace, right? What really counted was he loved her, no matter what he said or did.

She kept her silence during the ten-minute drive to the lake, aching inside at the gulf between them. But he'd had his explosion. She could feel him calming.

He drove across the grass and parked so they could look out over the water. Late afternoon sun sparkled on the lake. A duck glided silently toward shore, carving a V-shaped wake behind it. Hands tightly clasped, she glanced uneasily in Cliff's direction. He stared straight ahead, gripping the steering wheel. "I'm sorry. I'm sorry I blew up like that. I don't know why I do it! I didn't mean what I said. I just get so... Forgive me, Cone! Please!" He turned to her, appealing, voice gruff.

"Oh, Cliff!" She fell into his arms. "Of course! But don't do it again! I get so scared! I can't stand when you're angry with me! I think you don't love me anymore."

"Of course I do!" he said, apologizing with kisses. "But you just don't think how you look to others. Being in that building alone with Brian! Wearing those skimpy shorts! What are you trying to do? Come on to all the guys?"

"What?" She pulled back in surprise. Karen, with her long, shapely legs and short shorts, was the one who drew attention.

"Let's not argue again." Cliff drew her close, kissing

her forehead, her cheeks, her mouth, always most passionate after an argument. She tried to respond, but his criticism and physical attack still hurt. She had to bury the resentment if they were to go on together. If he didn't want her to wear shorts, okay. She'd wear jeans and a big shirt. No big deal. She'd wear a suit of armor, if that's what he wanted.

Driving home later, with Cliff's right hand on her bare knee, he told her about the plans he was making with his Y kids, told how he'd handled a fight between two boys. Alex closed her eyes, hearing him from afar, not quite trusting his good mood. She thought of sharing the happy session she'd had with Justin, but it might remind him of Brian and start things all over again. She worried how she'd explain not phoning about her lateness and hoped Dad was working late so he wouldn't know. Mom would take Cliff's side; Dad wouldn't.

"Now, about tonight," Cliff said as they approached home. "What do you say we go get some tacos? You can phone your folks from there..."

"I can't stay out." Alex touched his hand. "I told you. I'm sure I did. I promised Jenna I'd come over. We're supposed to work on plans for a kid's birthday party. Jenna got us the date and I promised to help."

Cliff snapped his forehead. "Oh, *yeah*!" Then he said, "But Cone, we're having such a good time now. Call her, put it off. You can see her tomorrow."

"I can't, Cliff."

"Why? Aren't we more important? Damn! She's using you! You're the creative one and she's just a drone. A loser! Why do you need her?" He took her hand and touched it to his face. "Come on, Cone. Call it off."

"We have so much to do to get ready. Things to plan, to buy, to rehearse. It's our first party! Cliff, really, I have to."

He dropped her hand. "You could do all that the day of the party! You're making such a big deal out of a dumb kid's party. If you really cared, you wouldn't want to be with anyone else, not even for a minute!"

"I *do* want to be with you, all the time. You know that...." Her voice shook. There she went again, talking back, defending herself, disappointing him. Why couldn't she be what he wanted? "All right," she said, softly. "I'll phone from the restaurant and figure out another time to get together, okay?"

Cliff gave her a crooked, happy grin. "That's my girl! Now let's go get us some tacos!"

TWELVE

"**So, what have you been**
up to?" Alex asked, trying to make conversation with
the friend she'd always talked easily to before. They
were on the way to the mall for the party supplies and
Jenna had hardly said a word since they left the house.

"Do you realize the party's tomorrow, and you've
left almost everything to me?" Jenna replied, ignoring
Alex's question. "I thought we were in this together! I've
had to buy most of the supplies, wrap the gifts, plan the
decorations, figure out the games to keep thirty wild
kids under control—all by myself! Where were you,
huh?"

"I'm sorry, Jenna, really. You know I'm not like that.
I couldn't help the other night."

"*Why*? What *are* you and Cliff—Siamese twins?
What could have been so important that he couldn't do
without you for a few hours?"

"You don't understand."

"Try me!"

"Sssh!" Alex whispered. They entered the lower level of the mall and moved with the crowds to the escalator. Jenna's angry voice drew attention.

"I didn't want to tell you on the phone with Cliff standing right there," she whispered. "We had a big argument, see? When we finally made up, I couldn't just run off and leave him like that, could I? He'd have felt I didn't really forgive him, see?" It hadn't really happened like that, but she didn't want Jenna to blame Cliff.

"Forgive him for what?"

"Oh..." How much dare she admit? Alex brushed a hand through the air to make light of what she'd said. "Nothing, really. Cliff's very possessive. He doesn't like me to talk to another guy." She smiled apologetically. "Guess he loves me a lot."

"That's *love*?" They had reached the novelty store and Jenna took Alex's arm to keep her from entering. "That's *control*! Cliff doesn't want you to talk to *anyone*, not just guys!"

"That's crazy!"

"Yeah? Why should you have to cut yourself off from all your friends just because he says so? Ever since you two started seeing each other you've dropped all your friends, not just me! What happens when you break up? Who'll be there to help pick up the pieces?"

Alex jerked her arm away. "That's even crazier than you said before. Cliff and I are like this!" She intertwined her fingers. "*Break up*? Not likely. You know what? I don't like this conversation!" She brushed past Jenna and marched into the store. "I thought you wanted me to help shop," she called over her shoulder, so furious that she didn't even try to sound cordial. "So? Come *on*!"

As they moved along the variety store aisles, deciding what party favors to buy, Alex found herself disliking Jenna's attitude more and more. She had no right to talk to her like that! Imagine, suggesting Cliff controlled her, that they'd eventually break up! The trouble with Jenna was that she'd never gone steady. She just didn't understand how things worked, how your boyfriend became your best friend now. If she had to choose between Cliff and Jenna, there was no question who it would be.

They hardly spoke as they shopped, except to confer on what to buy, and Jenna decided so slowly! It was getting late! Cliff said he'd phone, maybe come by. What if he was waiting?

"Look, I'm *sorry*," Jenna said, when they finally left the store. "I didn't mean to sound so critical, but we used to be friends and we were always honest with each other. I'm not jealous of you and Cliff. I just want a little of what we used to have." She backed against the wall to let people pass and Alex glanced quickly at her watch. "Sure, I have other friends, but it's not the same. I miss the talks, the fun we used to have. I really looked forward to us working together on these parties, and it's not happening like that."

"I miss you, too," Alex said. "Can we talk as we

walk? I really have to get home." She hurried along. "Things are different now, that's all." She pushed through the doors to the street, wishing Jenna would keep up. "Maybe you should find someone else to work with you on these parties. Between the Y job and Cliff, I don't seem to have time!"

When Jenna didn't answer, Alex quickly added, "We'll still be friends!"

"You haven't heard a word I said!"

"Don't be that way!" She felt an almost hysterical need to get home. Jenna didn't appreciate how hard she tried to find time for her. To avoid trouble, she hadn't even told Cliff about this shopping trip. Now, because it had taken so long, she couldn't even stay to help organize the party things for tomorrow.

"Look, Jenna," Alex said when they turned into their street. "You're right. I haven't done my share. I'll help out tomorrow, but whatever we're paid, you keep."

"No way!"

Alex's legs turned to jelly. Down the block, in front of her house, was Cliff's red Mustang. How long had he been waiting? She flew to Jenna's front door and deposited her packages on the landing. "Gotta go. Sorry. Cliff's waiting!"

"Let him!"

"I'll phone you tonight, bye!" She sprinted down the walk and across three lawns to her own house, like iron drawn to a magnet.

"Alex?" Jenna called after her.

"What?"

"Don't phone; I'll be busy! Oh—never mind!" She picked up the bags Alex had left and hurried into her home.

Alex charged into the house by the side door, stopped for an instant to catch her breath, then walked quickly through the kitchen toward the voices in the family room.

"Hi, guys!" she greeted as if all was normal. Kim and a friend were playing a board game at the table.

"Cliff's looking for you!" Kim announced.

Alex put a hand to her throat. "Where is he?"

"Outside. He came in for a while, but got tired of waiting. Said you should have told him where you'd be. Stacy, stop cheating! It's not your turn!"

Alex hurried from the room through the hall to the front door. Now, she was in for it.

"Alex, is that you?" her mother called. "Bring the mail in, will you, hon? We're upstairs."

She heard the music, Mozart, coming from her father's study. She saw the pile of mail dropped through the slot onto the entry hall floor. She picked up the mail and left it on the hall table, opened the front door, and ran down the path to Cliff's car.

"Hi!" She bent to look through the window to judge his mood. He was tapping the steering wheel impatiently.

"Hope you weren't waiting long," she said cheerily. She ran around the car, opened the door and climbed in, then threw her arms around Cliff's neck. "I had to shop with Jenna for the party tomorrow. It took forever. She's so slow making up her mind about everything, but we're all fixed now. I told her I couldn't do this anymore, that I don't have the time. She was really upset."

"Hold it!" Cliff pushed her away. "You're babbling again!" His grim look made her think that something else bothered him, something that had nothing to do with her.

"What's wrong?"

"Diane's run away!" Cliff glared at her.

"Your sister?" It took a second for the words to sink in. "Are you sure?"

"Sure I'm sure! Do you think I'd say it if I wasn't?" She shrank back a little, ashamed.

"When she didn't come to breakfast, Mom went in to wake her. Her bed hadn't been slept in and she wasn't there."

"Maybe she went jogging, or maybe she slept over at a friend's house and forgot to tell your parents!" Alex said, trying to ease his worry. "Did she take anything? Clothes?"

"Don't you think I thought of that? I *told* you—she's run away!" Cliff replied. "I've driven all over town looking for her. Nothing. I called her friends. Nothing. She could be on a bus to New York, for all I know!"

"Call the police!"

"And let the world know what happened?"

"But if…" Alex stopped at Cliff's warning look and tried another direction. "What about that guy she was seeing? Robert Lewis or something?"

Cliff drummed his fingers nervously on the steering wheel. "That clown? It's been over for months. Dad said he'd ground her for a year if she saw him again."

"But maybe she didn't listen," Alex offered, knowing she might be treading on dangerous ground.

Cliff frowned. "Maybe. It's worth a try." He started the car. "I tell you, if she's with him, she's in trouble, real trouble!"

Diane was a weird one, but why run away? Alex wondered as they drove through the quiet suburban streets toward the older part of town. Could life at home be that bad? She thought of that strange look Mr. Vandermeer had given her on graduation day and shivered.

"She's *crazy*," Cliff said, as if she'd asked. "She doesn't know how *good* she's got it. You wouldn't believe what she'll do to get Mom and Dad's goat. Like what she wears. She's got a closet full of nice clothes, but all you see her in is Salvation Army rejects. Sixties stuff. Yesterday, know what she did?"

Alex pressed her feet to the floor, braking, as Cliff drove through a red light, intent on his thoughts.

"She *butchered* her hair. I mean, butchered it! Can

you imagine?" Cliff's voice rose. "She cut all that long, gorgeous hair, lopped it off like you'd take a lawn mower to it. Now, is that crazy, or what?" There was a catch in his voice, like pain.

"Why would she do it?" Alex asked, anxiously eyeing the speedometer.

"Who knows?" Cliff's lips pressed together in a tight line. "She came down to show us and just stood there, gloating! Dad nearly blew a fuse. I think he wanted to kill her! I ask you, what's she got to run away for? Mom never asks a thing of her and Dad adores her. Okay, he's no angel, but with Diane, it's different. He treats her like a little princess, buys her gifts all the time, pays more attention to her than to Mom. What's she want to run away for?"

Treats Diane like a princess? Alex made a face. What about graduation day, when he insulted her in front of everyone, then squeezed her arm until she cringed. What about Diane's bitterness and cynicism? She thought of mentioning these things, of trying to defend Diane, but it might bring Cliff's anger down on her, so she kept silent.

The house Cliff drove to was in the poorer part of town. Graffiti covered the storefronts. What grass and few trees grew had a gray-black look from dust and thirst. Most cars on the street were old models, big, battered gas guzzlers.

"What are you going to do—if she's there?" Alex asked softly when Cliff shoved the gearshift into park and glared at the gray clapboard house ahead of them. Without answering, he jerked open the car door and jumped out.

Alex scurried after him, running to keep up. "Cliff, wait. What are you going to do?"

Cliff clomped up the three steps to the wooden porch and across it to the front door. He rapped his knuckles hard against the wood. "What am I going to do?" he repeated. "Get my sister, that's what! Just watch," he said, ominously. "Just watch!"

THIRTEEN

A girl of about ten answered the door. She had the same dark hair and eyes as Robert and held a baby in her arms. Two other children sat on a worn sofa, watching TV cartoons. The lemon scent of furniture polish blended with old cooking odors.

"Who is it, Terry?" a woman's voice called.

Cliff stepped forward. "I'm Cliff Vandermeer. Where's Diane? She's here, isn't she?"

"Cliff!" Alex whispered. She put a hand on his arm, but he shook it off.

Terry stepped back and her dark eyes widened. The baby began to wail.

"What do *you* want?" Robert came out of a dark hallway beyond the living room. He was not much taller than Diane and slight of build. "Go inside, Terry, it's okay. Go on," he said, moving between his sister and Cliff.

"Where's Diane?" Cliff demanded. "She came to you, didn't she?"

"Go home, Vandermeer. She doesn't want to see you!"

"Oh, no? We'll see!" Cliff shoved Robert out of his way, crossed the room and started down the hall. "Diane? Diane, where are you?"

"Cliff, don't!" Alex whispered. "This isn't right. Let's go!" She held on to the back of his shirt, following wherever he went but feeling more and more uncomfortable.

Robert leaped in front of Cliff and danced back and forth to keep him from moving on.

Cliff pushed him aside. "I ought to flatten you, creep! You were warned to stay away from my sister. Where is she?"

"What *is* this?" A small, thin woman came out of a back room. "Who are you? What do you want?" Hands on hips, she blocked their way.

"I'm Diane's brother. I'm here to take her home!"

"This is *my* house! You leave now, or I call the police!" the woman said, but Cliff ignored her, pushing open doors as he advanced down the hall. "Diane? Diane? Come out right now, or I'll cream that boyfriend of yours!"

"Cliff, *please*," Alex tugged at his shirt. "Let's go now, please!"

"Go home! Leave me alone!" Diane pushed by Mrs. Lewis. "And don't you dare hurt Bobby!"

Alex bit her lip. Diane looked terrible. Her hair was an uneven stubble and she wore big, dark glasses like some of the druggies at school did.

"Go away!" Diane cried. "Leave me alone!"

"She stays—if she wants!" Mrs. Lewis put an arm around Diane.

"Keep out of this, lady!" Cliff snarled. "Get your things, Di! You've caused enough trouble. I want you outta here, now."

"Please come with us, Diane," Alex urged. "Your parents are really worried."

"No!" Diane covered her face and shook her head.

"Diane…" Alex said, resisting the urge to reach out and comfort her.

"Look!" Diane tore off her sunglasses. The right eye was swollen and half closed. "See how worried they are! Is this what I should go back to? Huh?"

"Oh!" Alex cried, stepping back.

"Shut up, Di! Damn it, shut up!" Cliff glanced around. "I've had enough of your craziness. Get your things and let's go, now!"

"You heard her, Vandermeer!" Robert stepped between Cliff and his sister. "She doesn't want to go so get outta my house and leave us alone."

"Stay out of this!" Cliff made a sound like an angry lion. Suddenly he sprang at Robert, lifted him off the floor and pinned him against the wall.

Mrs. Lewis screamed. The younger children cried, then attacked Cliff with fists and teeth. Alex pulled at his arm. "Cliff, stop it! Leave him alone! Please—let's go!"

"*Stop it!* Stop it! All of you!" Diane shouted above the bedlam. She stood in the hallway with hands jammed tightly over her ears. Tears rolled down her cheeks. "Stop it! Leave Bobby alone! I'll go!"

"Di, no! You don't have to!" Robert wiped at his bloody nose.

"It's no use, Bobby. I'm sorry I got you into this. I wish…" Diane's voice dropped and she gestured hopelessly.

"Go *with* her, Alex," Cliff ordered. "See she gets her things and doesn't try to climb out the window or something! Go on, you heard me!"

Alex hesitated, then obeyed. If only she hadn't come along. If only she'd never reminded Cliff about Robert. She followed Diane into a room, glancing backward in hopes of a reprieve. If was awful, what they were doing. Cliff had been so aggressive, so physical! It was awful to come into Bobby's house and order everyone around! Yet she could almost understand. Diane ran away. Cliff always stood between her and their father. He'd been all over town hunting for her. He was scared. Maybe he expected he'd be blamed for her disappearance.

Alex leaned against a chest of drawers while Diane gathered clothes and stuffed them into a backpack. She tried not to watch; it made her feel like a jailor. "I'm sorry, Diane. I hate this. I know Cliff got all crazy but it's because he really loves you. He's afraid to go home without you. He didn't mean to hurt Robert. You know how he is when he gets angry. He loves you."

"*Love?*" Diane's voice cracked.

"I don't know why you ran away but I'm sure you can work it out."

Diane swung around suddenly. "What do *you* know?" She pointed to her swollen black eye and the bruised cheekbone below. "That's how they work things out at the Vandermeer house!"

Alex stared at the bruises, unable to think how to answer. Embarrassed, she turned to look at a rock concert poster until Diane finished packing, then led the way back out to the hall.

"Good-bye, Mama Lewis," Diane said, hugging Robert's mother. She touched Robert's face with a finger, then strode quickly out the door to where Cliff waited beside the car.

Alex huddled away from Cliff, wary and uneasy. Something was terribly wrong. All she saw lately was Cliff's aggressive side. Where was that other person she loved? What went on in his home? Couldn't he do anything about it? Poor Diane.

"Put your seat belt on!" Cliff growled, eyeing his sister through the rearview mirror.

Alex flinched.

Diane clicked her seat belt on, but it seemed she didn't really care what happened to her.

"Damn it, Di! What'd you do to set him off this time! Why didn't you come to me?" Cliff glanced anxiously at his sister in the rearview mirror. "Can't you just try to fit in?"

Diane stared out the window, almost as if she wasn't listening.

"Listen, sis," Cliff said gently, then more forcefully as Diane didn't turn his way. They had almost reached Alex's house. "Be smart. When we get home don't start in again. It won't do any good. Just apologize, okay? They're really worried. Dad even thought you might have done something stupid, like hurt yourself."

"Next time, I will."

Alex swung around to see if Diane meant what she said.

"You'll be out of the house in a few years, Di. Play his game because you can't win. I can take it, why can't you?" Cliff asked.

"I'm *tired* of taking it. I hate him! I don't know why you put up with it either, the way he puts you down!"

Cliff slammed his hand on the steering wheel. "There you go again! You don't give up, do you!"

Diane turned her face back to the window.

When Cliff parked in front of Alex's home to let her off, Alex stretched back to touch Diane's hand. It was cold and damp. "Don't worry, Di," she said. "They'll be so glad you're safe they'll forget everything else. Just watch. You'll be okay. And Di? If you want to talk, call me. I mean it."

"Yeah." Diane nodded. "I'll be all right. As you said,

my father really *loves* me. Everyone should be so loved!"

Alex frowned. Sarcasm again. Diane wasn't easy to like.

"See you tonight?" Alex asked Cliff as she left the car. "You'll let me know what time?"

"Yeah." Cliff tapped the steering wheel with a finger, staring straight ahead.

"Bye, Diane."

"Bye." Diane didn't look at her either.

FOURTEEN

While waiting for Cliff's
call, Alex tried to concentrate on the story she'd tell at
the party Sunday. But her mind skipped from worry to
worry. She replayed every minute of what happened at
Robert's house in the morning and almost persuaded
herself that Cliff was not a villain but a hero. Maybe he
overreacted in trying to rescue Diane, but he meant well.
She worried how Cliff made out when he brought Diane
home. Would Mr. Vandermeer go after him? The afternoon dragged by with no phone calls. She considered
asking Jenna over to discuss last-minute party details
but put it off. If Cliff arrived, Jenna would have to leave.

By late afternoon a knot in her throat grew so big
and hard that she could hardly swallow. Was Cliff angry
with her? Had she spoken out of turn? Was he ground-
ed? Why didn't he phone? By six thirty she was so anxious she considered calling him, but Cliff said the
Vandermeers laughed at girls who had phoned him in
the past. They said they were not "ladies." Restless to

the point of nausea, she wandered downstairs.

Her mother glanced up from the stove, where she was fixing dinner for guests. "You look nice, honey. That sweater is very becoming."

"Thanks."

"Where's Cliff? Weren't you going to dinner and a movie? Shouldn't he be here by now?"

"I thought so, but he hasn't called." She nibbled a carrot stick, trying to look unconcerned, but her voice gave her away.

Mrs. Cummings emptied a bag of potstickers into a pot of hot oil. "You're letting him take you for granted, honey. Maybe you should date other boys."

"No, I *shouldn't*!"

Her mother lowered the fire and turned to Alex. "It's a fact of life, sweetie. Men appreciate women more when they have competition."

"Oh, *Mom*!" she exploded. "We don't play *games*! I can't date someone just to make Cliff jealous! I can't! You just don't understand!" She stalked out of the kitchen with her mother calling after her and ran back to her room to flop face down on the bed. She pressed her face into the pillow feeling desolate, as if someone had cut a deep hole in her heart. Cliff had to come! He wouldn't just leave her waiting without calling.

When at last she heard Cliff's car, she jumped up, grabbed her purse and flew down the stairs, filled with relief and anxiety.

"We're late. Let's go," Cliff said as soon as she opened the door to him.

"We're going!" she called out to her mother and hurried to the car after Cliff. "Where were you? Why didn't you call? I was so worried!"

"Don't start in, Cone! I'm here, aren't I?" He slid into the driver's seat and plugged the key in the ignition. "Buckle up and let's go."

She fixed her safety belt, then glanced sideways at him and said, "Hi…"

"Hi!" He patted her hand.

"Like my new sweater?" It was a gray-green with pink and white flowers, like suspenders, down the front. As soon as she'd seen it she loved it, and she was sure Cliff would, too.

He gave her a critical once-over, frowned, and started out of the driveway.

"You don't like it?"

"The color's all wrong for you. Puke green! And— those flowers down the front! Straight out of *The Sound of Music*."

She reached for the door handle. "Go back. Give me two minutes and I'll change."

"Don't be silly. We're late!"

"No, I want to. Please, turn around! I'll feel self-conscious all evening now!"

He drove on down the street. "Don't make such a big thing of it! Just don't wear it again, okay? Keep your jacket on if you feel embarrassed." He mouthed a kiss. "Poor Cone…"

She hugged her arms around herself, feeling miserable.

"I got a new tape. Listen." Cliff plugged in a cassette and turned the volume up. He nodded to the music.

"Are you late because of Diane?" she asked.

"No. Isn't this group great?"

"What happened when you got home? How'd it go with your parents?"

He grimaced. "It's a long story. I don't want to talk about it now."

"Oh." She looked at her watch. No time to eat. "Did you have dinner?"

"Yeah. You?"

"Just a carrot stick. I thought we'd be eating together."

"Sorry, Cone. After I got Diane home some guys called and we went bowling. Then we wound up at Domino's and ran into Karen and some of the kids from the Y. I wanted to call, but time just flew. You know how it goes." He smiled as if remembering something pleasant. "If you're hungry, I'll get some popcorn."

The knot in her throat grew harder. All those hours she had waited and worried and he'd been with his friends, with *Karen*, having fun.

"What's wrong? You're not *angry*, are you?" He frowned at her.

"I guess you'd have called if you could."

"You know I would! I'm not inconsiderate!"

They sat in the back of the movie theater and later she couldn't really say what the film was about. With Cliff holding her close, his lips on hers and his hands caressing her in the dark, she could only feel the heat and yearning that he always aroused in her. At times like this she knew for sure that Cliff loved her. He whispered again and again how much, as they kissed, and she believed him. For now, at least, that was all that mattered.

"Hey, Cliff! Alex, wait!"

They were leaving the theater after the show. Alex felt a rosy contentment, ambling along with Cliff's arm protectively around her.

"It's Mark and Julie," Cliff said. "If they want to join us, make some excuse, okay? We want to be alone." He gave Alex a meaningful smile. "Right?"

"Right," she said, after a second's hesitation. She knew what he intended for the rest of the evening. They'd start making out and pretty soon he'd want her to let him do more and she'd stop him. "Damn it, why?" he'd ask, frustrated. "Everyone does it. We've been going together forever and you know I love you! Why?" Because it was such a huge step, one she wasn't ready for, she'd say. Because she was afraid and needed to be sure. "It's okay," he'd say, reluctantly backing off. "I can wait, but it's not easy!"

"You guys want to go for a burger with us?" Mark asked as soon as he and Julie caught up.

Julie ran fingers through her blond hair as she eyed Cliff.

"What do you say, Alex?" Cliff asked, as if it was up to her. "You hungry?"

A hunger pang rumbled in her stomach, but she said, "Not very. And it's kind of late."

"Yeah. Gotta get Alex home before she turns into a pumpkin." Cliff squeezed her affectionately and Alex smiled weakly; Julie rolled her eyes and Mark laughed. And then the two boys began discussing the movie.

"I love your sweater," Julie said. "Where'd you get it? The color's great on you."

"You really think so?" Alex stood straighter. "My mother likes it too, but Cliff doesn't."

Cliff swung around. "Doesn't like *what*?"

"Oh, nothing," she stammered in the sudden awkward silence.

"Come on, what don't I like?"

Alex squirmed. "My sweater."

"Oh, that! Right. The color! Puke green. But Alex likes it; that's all that matters." He tightened his arm around her waist. It was a signal.

"Gotta go, guys," Alex said. "Sorry we can't join you, but next time, maybe."

"She's the boss!" Cliff shrugged, as if he would have stayed had it been his choice.

Alex forced a smile and let him lead her away.

"That wasn't fair," she said as they walked to his car. She'd debated these last minutes whether to bring up how he made her feel in front of the others. Maybe it wasn't serious enough to risk his anger, but how could she be loving now when he criticized her taste in clothes, called her silly, and told others *she* was controlling?

"What wasn't fair?" Cliff unlocked the car on her side and held the door for her. "How can I be unfair when I love you so much?" There was a gentleness to his tone and a tender, vulnerable look in his eyes. She sensed that if ever she could get him to change, it had to be at a time like this when he wanted her so much.

"Cliff, listen." She gently pushed him away when he tried to draw her close.

He raised his arms in surrender, then crossed them over his chest and grinned. "I'm listening. Speak, O great Cone-love!"

He was teasing, not really listening, but she had to try to make him understand. "I don't mean to criticize, but it's not fair that you blamed our having to leave on me," she said.

Cliff's eyes widened in mock surprise and he leaned back on his heels as if she had struck him.

"I'm serious, Cliff. Please don't make a joke of this."

"Come on, 'lex. I thought you'd be flattered that I

left those guys thinking you're the boss. Man—it made *me* look bad, *me* look like a wimp letting *you* call the shots!"

Was it possible? Had she misread the way Julie and Mark took what he said? He so often confused her, making her doubt what she perceived and accept his view of things.

"Anything else?" Cliff put his hands on her shoulders.

He was being so nice that she decided to go on. "I felt awful when you told Mark and Julie that I might turn into a pumpkin. A *pumpkin*!"

"Boy, are you sensitive! Where's your sense of humor? I was just *kidding*! You should know that!"

"You used me to get a laugh! You made me feel ugly!"

"Aw, come on! I tell you all the time you're beautiful, don't I?" He tried to draw her close but she stiffened.

"Not *more*?"

"Did you have to call my sweater *puke* green—in front of everyone? I mean, you know how embarrassed I felt about wearing it after you said you didn't like it! I *wanted* to change before we left, but..." She stopped, realizing by the turn of his lips that she'd gone too far.

"That's enough. If you don't like my sense of humor, tough. From the minute I picked you up it's been nag, nag nag! Who needs it? Come on, I'll take you home."

Cliff pushed her so she fell against the car, and strode away.

She pressed a hand against her back and ran after him. "Cliff, wait!" She'd been crazy to make a fuss over something so trivial. *He* didn't need her. He could have anyone he wanted. Karen, Julie, other girls. Where would that leave her? She swallowed her pride and grabbed his sleeve as he climbed in the car. "Wait, I'm sorry! Honestly. Please, I'm sorry."

He frowned, considering, and seemed to reach a decision. "All right. Get in," he said.

She hurried around the car and climbed in, wanting to ask, Is everything okay now? Am I forgiven? You're not taking me home, are you? But she didn't ask. Instead, she buckled her seat belt hurriedly and faced forward. Her heart raced and a hard lump of tears lay like undigested food in her chest.

It wasn't until Cliff drove up toward the hills, toward their private make-out place, that she knew it would be all right. He'd forgiven her. But it would cost. Fear tingled through her fingers and up into her arms. Now, because she'd made him angry, he'd want—no, he'd *expect* her to make it up to him. While part of her longed for reassurance in his arms, a greater part felt resistant, even frighteningly repulsed.

"I'm tired and hungry," she said softly. "Maybe we should go home."

Cliff took the turnoff to the mountains. "Why? Ten

minutes ago you complained that you didn't want to!"

"I have a party tomorrow and I have to be up early."

"Don't worry. I'll have you home early enough."

She drew in a scared breath, squeezed her hands between her knees, and nodded.

FIFTEEN

"**Y**ou were going to tell me what happened when you got home with Diane," Alex said, trying to postpone what they'd come up here for, at least long enough so she'd feel more loving.

"Diane…" Cliff said with distaste.

He had driven off the road to the dirt turnoff. The car bumped over the rough surface and came to a stop near the edge of the canyon where they could look down on the lights of the city. A warm, sweet breeze came through the open windows. Alex crossed her arms over her chest and leaned away from Cliff.

"Why was Diane so scared to go home? Would your dad hit her? How did she get that black eye? What happened?"

Cliff placed a hand on her leg and gave her the soft half-smile that always led to making out. "Not now, Cone. That can wait. Let's get in back. It's too cramped here."

She edged against the car door, hands trembling. Part of her hungered for this closeness his loving would bring, but not now. Not feeling as she did about the way he behaved at Robert's house. About how he pushed her around. She seemed to be moving the boundaries of what she accepted further and further out. What was normal and how much should she allow?

She was beginning to feel used, even *abused*. What else could she call it? No matter what she said or did or how she dressed or rearranged her life to please him, he found fault. And when she didn't measure up, he belittled or hit her. Expecting the next blowup kept her on edge and made her feel hopelessly inadequate.

"Come on, Cone. In back..." Cliff touched her arm.

In a kind of shock, obeying out of habit rather than desire, she forced herself to move out of the car, push the seat forward and climb in back. Cliff vaulted over his seat and held out his arms.

She moved into his embrace but hid her face against his chest. His heart beat against her ear, hard and fast, and his aftershave, which normally made her weak with longing, sickened her. If only she could relax, let him kiss her a while, she might feel different.

"Hey, Cone, relax! You're stiff as a board!" Cliff lifted her face with one hand and gazed at her. "Tears? Cripes! *Now*, what?"

She turned her face away. "I just don't feel like doing this now. Let's go back."

"Damn it, Alexandra! What's your problem? You've been a drag all evening."

Alex drew back and gazed out the window. "Sometimes I feel like you don't really love me, like all you want is to make out."

"That's ridiculous. We spend lots of time together doing other things, you know that! I do love you. I need you. You're beautiful. You're terrific. Okay? Enough? Now, come here."

Alex pressed her body against the door frame, as far from Cliff as she could get. "I can't," she whispered. "I just can't!" She stared hard at him, scared at how he'd react.

"Maybe *you* can't, but I *can*!" He slid over and drew her to him. "Quit playing games, Alex; I'm out of patience. You come on to me, get me all steamed up, and cry 'Stop, Stop!' That's enough! You want it. You know you do."

"No!" She clamped her lips tight and struggled to break free, suddenly frightened.

"Don't fight me, Cone. Come on, love..." He pressed his lips against hers and tried to pull her away from the door.

"Don't!" She gasped. "No!"

"Why, you—" He drew back and touched his lip. "You bit me! You hurt me, damn it!" He jerked her toward him and pushed her down on the seat. "That's it! I didn't want to hurt you, but you're going to do what I say!" He grabbed her arms and held them, then bent and kissed her face and neck.

She was crying now, almost sick with fear and revulsion. He was going to do it and she couldn't stop him. She saw the passion-dimmed eyes as if his brain was already turned off, heard the fast intakes of breath as he bent over her.

"No, no! Oh, please Cliff!" she begged. "I don't want to. Don't! Don't!" She twisted from side to side, squirmed this way and that, terrified, but he was much stronger and heavier than she.

"I want you," Cliff hissed, breathing hard. "I've wanted you so long!" His words came in gasps. "It'll be okay. Don't fight. Relax... Cone... Cone..." He yanked at her jeans and forced them down over her legs, cursing her for fighting.

It wasn't supposed to be like this! She'd fantasized so often about this special moment. They'd be somewhere romantic and he'd be so loving, so full of tenderness and wonder. She'd want to give herself because he needed her so much, because she loved him with all her heart.

It wasn't supposed to be like this! She was an animal in a trap, biting, scratching, crying to get out. Her heart beat wildly and she stared in horror at this figure looming over her, struggling to undo his pants. "Don't! Don't!" she screamed, pushing with both hands against him.

He slapped her. "That's enough! I told you!"

Finally, sobbing, eyes tightly shut, she gave up.

Let him. What difference did it make?

*　　*　　*　　*　　*

Afterward, drained, hurting inside, sick to her stomach, she sat up and plucked her clothes from the floor. Silently, unable to look at Cliff, she began to dress. Cliff's face was flushed, his breathing quick and heavy. He patted her arm, then climbed back to the driver's seat and started the engine. He swung the car around, drove off the gravel to the road, and then headed down the hill toward home.

She felt so terribly cold. Huddled against the door frame, she hugged herself and stared at the dark beyond the window. Trees and bushes went by, black shadows momentarily lit by the headlights.

"Come on, Cone. Don't act like I'm a monster. You knew we'd do it sometime," Cliff said from the front seat, checking her frequently in the rearview mirror. They were getting close to home.

She pressed her cheek against the cold glass window and didn't answer. It felt wet and sticky between her legs. It hurt.

"It's *your* fault, you know! Why'd you fight like that? I'd never have hit you. I'm sorry it wasn't good for you. Next time it'll be better."

She pulled her legs up under her, moving deeper into the back seat corner, wanting to disappear.

"Come on, 'lex," he urged. "Don't cry. We'll be home soon and you don't want your folks seeing you all red-eyed and stuff."

When she still didn't answer he said, "Damn it, 'lex, what do you want me to say? I'm sorry, *okay?* I'm sorry! I got carried away. I couldn't help it." He sounded contrite, but angry, too. "You turn me on so much, I go out of my mind! What do you expect?"

Her teeth began to chatter. "I'm cold," she whispered. All she wanted was to get home, shower, climb into bed and draw the blankets over her head. She wanted to sleep forever so she wouldn't have to remember what just happened.

SIXTEEN

Sunday. **She awoke to** the sounds of a mockingbird's trill and muffled voices from the TV downstairs. She had slept like the dead, blocking out everything, but now it all came back. The images of last night rolled across the screen behind her eyes without pause. She groaned, drew the blanket around her, and stuffed the sheet into her mouth.

A knock came at her door. "Alex? Alex, honey? Wake up!" It was her mother. "It's after eight. You said you wanted to be at Jenna's house by nine!" The door swung open and her mother stuck her head inside. "Hi, sweetie. It's so hot today! How come you're so bundled up? You sick?" She came to the bed and placed a hand on Alex's forehead. "Oh, my! What happened to your lip?"

Alex touched her swollen lip and winced. "It's nothing. I... I...was chewing something and... bit it." She closed her eyes and fought back the urge to cry, to tell her mother all that had happened.

"Are you and Cliff…?" Alex could read her mother's mind. She thought the lip was due to heavy kissing. "Never mind. I'll get something—a wash cloth, antiseptic!" She hurried to the bathroom.

"No, Mom, *please*!" she called. "Go away! I'll take care of it myself! Mom—leave it alone!"

Her mother returned with an ice cube wrapped in a cloth. She sat on the bed and pressed the cloth against Alex's lip. "You look terrible, you know that? How do you feel?"

"So-so. It's just my period starting, that's all. Don't worry, Mom." Her voice nearly broke.

"I don't know. Maybe your father's right. Maybe you're too young to be dating only one boy. What time did you get in?"

She took the cloth from her mother and forced a reassuring smile. "Before midnight! Honest. Go on, Mom. I'll be okay. Be downstairs in a minute."

When her mother left, she eased out of bed and went to the bathroom to look in the mirror. A corner of her mouth was swollen and caked with dry blood. She found a dark bruise on her right upper arm, where Cliff had punched her, and elsewhere, too. It hurt as if she'd been cut with a knife between her legs.

She leaned on the sink, bent her head, and sobbed as if her heart had burst. Oh, God. What should she do? How could Cliff have done that? How could he? She'd said no, begged him to stop. Why wouldn't he? How could he hit her, force her? She turned on the shower so no one would hear her sobs.

He said it was *her* fault, that she teased him, led him on till he couldn't stop. It wasn't true! Even if it was—he had no right! A fresh wave of tears poured out.

She gagged as a wave of nausea bubbled up. Now what? Was she pregnant? Did you know so soon? Bent over the sink, she began to retch. Her whole stomach seemed to be turning inside out. Perspiration seeped from every pore, running down her forehead, arms, and neck, and tears slid down her cheeks.

"Alex? Alex!" Kim called, jiggling the locked knob. "Are you sick? I'll get Mom!"

She held a hand over her mouth and called in a voice strange to her ears, "I'm okay! Just go away!"

"I'm telling Mom," Kim cried, already running, calling down the hall to her mother.

Choking back sobs, Alex scrubbed at the mess in the sink, rinsed her mouth and slapped water on her face. If her mother saw her like this there'd be *more* questions. Questions she didn't want to answer. She yanked off her nightshirt and hurriedly climbed into the shower.

"Let me in, Alex! Open the door!" her mother called.

"What?"

"Alex, open this door right now!"

"I can't!" she called back, her voice disguised by the force of the water. "I'll be out soon!"

"Kim says you're sick! Open the door!"

"I can't!"

When her mother didn't reply, Alex figured she was waiting at the door, listening. It didn't matter. With the water running, she could cry as hard as she wanted, and Mom could never hear.

"You are *not* going out. I don't care what you say. You are not well enough to help Jenna at that party!"

Alex had dressed and air-blown her long hair, and now she sat in the kitchen, a cup of black coffee in hand. She felt trembly, empty and detached, ready to hide in the clown costume and engage the children at the party, ready to put aside everything except what the day demanded. Cleaned up, the cut on her lip didn't look too bad. "Mom," she said, patiently. "I have to go. We agreed to do this weeks ago and Jenna can't handle it alone. There'll be thirty kids!"

"Kim said you were throwing up!"

"I was, but I'm okay now. It must have been that taco I ate last night." She forced a smile. The only food she'd had was a small bag of popcorn. "Besides, you know how Kim exaggerates. She cries wolf all the time."

"I do not!" Kim exclaimed.

"Do so."

"Do not!"

She'd managed to change the subject and winked at her sister to show her she was teasing. "Gotta go!" She rose slowly from the table to avoid pain and reached for the cellophane-wrapped clown costume and game-filled canvas bag she'd brought downstairs. "Dad playing golf today?" She pecked her mother on the cheek.

"Take some Tylenol. Wait, I'll get it for you."

The phone rang. For an instant Alex stood very still, holding her breath, a surge of electricity racing down her arms and legs. Then she said, "Don't need it, Mom. Thanks. Gotta go." She raced to the door. "If that's Cliff, tell him I left," she called over her shoulder. Outside, she took a deep breath and almost stumbled in her hurry to get away.

It was all business at Jenna's house, not even a friendly word to show yesterday's meeting was forgotten. Her friend had already loaded the family van and found space for Alex's bag and costume. "I'll call out what we're taking and you check it off," Jenna said, handing Alex a pad. "Here goes. Fifty balloons, helium tank. Paper plates. Spoons, knives, and forks. Napkins. Tablecloths. Favors... You're not writing!" Jenna exclaimed. "How come?"

Alex shuddered, bent over the pad and said, "Napkins... er, tablecloths... What was that last thing?" Cliff's face looming above her, full of passion and determination, had momentarily flashed through her mind.

"Favors," Jenna said. "You okay? You look awful."

"I'm fine."

Jenna pursed her lips and turned away. "Dad? We're ready! Can you drive us now?"

As they carried boxes of party supplies into the Morgans' backyard Alex found Jenna eyeing her.

"What happened to your lip? And how'd you get those marks on your arms?" Jenna asked as they started unpacking the boxes.

"I fell."

A disbelieving smile flitted over her face. "Oh, right. Cliff had nothing to do with it, huh? I hear he can get pretty mean."

Alex's legs nearly gave way.

"How's it going, girls?"

"Mrs. Morgan!" Jenna turned to greet a woman crossing the lawn, leading a little girl. "Hi, big birthday girl! I'm Jenna. This is my friend, Alex. We're going to give you the funnest party you ever had."

Mrs. Morgan held her hand out to Alex. "Nice to meet you, dear. Do you have everything? Are the tables and chairs the way you want?"

"They're fine, Mrs. Morgan. You just relax. By noon we'll have everything ready. Right, Alex?"

"Right!"

"Then I'll see you both later. If you need anything, I'll be inside."

As soon as Mrs. Morgan and her daughter left they got to work. Jenna began unloading the boxes and Alex started blowing up the balloons. For the next several hours Alex tried not to think, but the hurt of last night kept returning.

As she and Jenna strung crepe paper to trees, she thought, I can't stand it! He shouldn't have! How can I have anything to do with him anymore? As she tied balloons to gates and bushes, she thought, He didn't even think he'd done wrong! She set tables, put out favors, and planned where to set up the games, and inwardly cried. *It should never have happened!*

Shortly before noon Mrs. Morgan returned to the yard. "Oh, my! This is beautiful!" She clapped her hands and gazed around. "You've done wonders! I never thought my boring yard could look so good! You're marvelous!"

Alex smiled. "Jenna deserves all the credit, Mrs. Morgan. She's a genius at planning and organizing!"

"Oh, no! It's Alex! *She's* the artistic one," Jenna said.

Mrs. Morgan nodded. "I can see why you two are such good friends. Just look, Taylor!" She put an arm around her little girl's shoulders. "I'd better get the camera so I can capture all this before the barbarians arrive!"

"And I'd better get into my clown costume," Alex said. "It's nearly time for the guests."

At four o'clock the last happy child departed, clutching a balloon and small toy. Alex and Jenna cleaned up all the party mess and packed away their own supplies. They collected the check for their purchases and service, plus a twenty dollar bonus. They sat at the curb waiting for Jenna's father to arrive to drive them home.

"It did go well," Jenna said. "Didn't it?"

"Yes, it really did," Alex agreed. "Thirty little kids and not one tantrum and hardly any tears. That's a miracle! But I'm exhausted."

Jenna plunked herself down on the curb. "Me too."

Alex leaned against a lamppost. "Did you see Taylor's face when I had the puppets sing 'Happy Birthday' to her? Pure rapture!"

"Yeah." Jenna smiled. "Want to hang around my house a while? Eat some yummy birthday cake Mrs. Morgan gave us?" She gazed hopefully at Alex. "I guess not. You'll want to get home to Cliff."

"No!" Alex said, quickly. "I'd love to stay, really."

"All *right*!" Jenna jumped up and hugged her. "We can figure out how to spend our fortune!" She waved the check at Alex and then stared at it. "Imagine! A twenty-dollar bonus! We *must* be good!"

"The best!" Alex said. And then, suddenly, without warning, last night's memories flooded back. And with it came the realization that she should never have anything to do with Cliff again. She burst into tears. How could she give him up? She still loved him. But how could she forgive him?

SEVENTEEN

"**Do you want to talk?**"
Jenna asked. "You don't have to, if you'd rather not, you know."

There'd been no time to explain her tears. Jenna's father arrived as Alex wiped her eyes, then when they reached home, Jenna's mother plied them with questions about the party. Now, Alex sat on a beanbag chair in her friend's bedroom clutching a plush gray-and-white Babar elephant while Jenna lay face down on her bed, watching.

"It's Cliff, isn't it?" Jenna prompted.

Alex hid her face in Babar's soft crown. How could she tell Jenna or *anyone* what happened? It was too shameful, too awful, too unbelievable. If she did speak, she didn't know where to begin, how much to tell, or even what she really felt. Her feelings shifted minute by minute. Maybe it hadn't really happened, or maybe it happened differently from how she remembered. Maybe, if she gave Cliff a chance, he'd apologize in a way she could accept.

"I have to work this out myself, Jen," Alex said, aware of her friend's unwavering gaze.

"I understand, but you always say it's better to talk things out and we always did. If that's what you want, though, what can I say?" Jenna sighed. "I just think something awful must have happened for you to cry like that."

Alex shut her eyes, afraid Jenna's kindness would start the tears again.

"Look. It can't be that bad. Have you broken up? Is that what it is? Did he hit you? Is that what? *Tell* me!"

"I *can't*."

"Yes, you can!"

Alex plucked at the fuzz on Babar's golden crown. After a moment she said, "It's hard. Will you promise not to tell a soul? Not a living soul?"

"Alex! You know I can keep a secret!"

She looked up, tears brimming in her eyes. "He... he..."

She couldn't go on.

Jenna waited.

"Cliff... raped me," she whispered.

"What?" Jenna jumped up and sat back on the edge of the bed. "What?"

Alex dropped her eyes. Her voice was low, full of pain. "We went to a movie last night and I was feeling really down because—because of lots of things I don't even want to get into." She clutched Babar tightly against her chest. "After the movie I told him about some of the ways he hurt me and he got angry. He drove up to—where we often go. I wanted to go home but Cliff insisted." She rubbed her eyes and looked at Jenna. "Whenever I'm angry or hurt, Cliff thinks making out will solve everything. *He* gets turned on and *I* get turned off. And we wind up doing what he wants."

Jenna leaned forward, her face expressionless.

"He's been pushing me to have sex." She glanced up quickly, then down again. "We've talked about it a lot and I always put him off. You know how I feel. It's such a big step. Well..." Just knowing the words coming next brought a knifelike pain to her heart.

"He wouldn't listen! Oh, Jenna! He wouldn't wait. He wouldn't! I kept saying no, but he wouldn't stop!" Tears flooded down her face and she shook with sobs. "I fought him. I did! I really tried!"

"Oh, Alex... Alex..." Jenna jumped off the bed, yanked a handful of tissues from a box on the bedstand, and squatted on the floor before her. "Oh, Alex..." she murmured.

"He—he—" A new spasm of tears burst from her chest.

Jenna tried clumsily to hug her. "I know, I know. Oh, Alex, I'm sorry. So sorry. Did you tell your parents? Did you see a doctor? Are you okay?"

"No, no! I couldn't! I couldn't tell anyone. You're the only one!"

"Tell them. You can't let him get away with it. You should go to the police!"

"No! You don't understand!" Alex pulled away and leaped to her feet. "He's not a *criminal*! He's not *really* a rapist! I should never have told you. I can't report him! Who'd believe me? People already assume we're doing it! No, I couldn't!" She stared in misery at Jenna and then, head down, added, "Anyway, it was probably as much my fault as his!"

"*Your* fault?" Jenna blocked Alex's way out of her room. "Quit defending him! Are you nuts?"

Alex glanced anxiously toward the hall and lowered her voice. "What if it's true what he said—that I tease him, lead him on, then make him stop?"

"You listen to me! It was *not* your fault! He's a bully! He decides who you see, what you wear, how you think, checks on you all the time, puts you down. Don't you see it? He's been leading up to this since you started going with him! For heaven's sake!"

The harsh ring of the phone jolted Alex, drew her attention beyond Jenna to the hall. She knew it was Cliff, as surely as if an umbilical cord connected them.

"Alex?" Jenna's mother called. "It's for you! Cliff!"

"You're *not* going to talk to him!" Jenna said as Alex pushed by to get to the door. "Don't, Alex. Be smart."

Cliff probably felt awful about what he did. Maybe he couldn't sleep all night, furious at himself for what he'd done, terrified that she wouldn't forgive him. Maybe he had some explanation she could accept.

Jenna flew after her and grabbed her arm. "Don't!"

Alex yanked free. "Leave me alone! I have to!"

"Yes?" She could barely get the word out as she pressed the receiver close to her ear. Her legs quaked and her breathing sounded like she'd just run five miles.

"It's me, Alex." Silence. "You okay?"

She held a hand over her mouth to silence the whimper.

"How'd the party go? I want to hear all about it."

A pounding began in her head so she couldn't think. Party? So often she didn't react to words or events until later, when she was alone and could sort out if she'd been injured in some way. Even then she always found reasons to blame herself rather than the other person. But now... she saw immediately how weird it was for Cliff to ask about the party after what had happened.

"So? How'd it go? You and Jenna pull it off? What do you say I come by and you tell me all about it? Fifteen minutes, your house, okay?"

She couldn't see him again, couldn't! Her lips moved but no words came out.

"Cone? You hear? We'll go out to dinner. I made reservations at that Chinese place you like. I have a surprise for you!"

"No!"

"Come on, Cone. I'm sorry about last night. I was

wrong. I know it wasn't how it should have been. It'll never happen again. Please—forgive me."

It'll never happen again. His favorite words. She shivered and wiped cold, wet hands against her jeans.

"Oh, shoot! We'd have done it sooner or later, you know that. If I hurt you, I'm really sorry. I just couldn't help myself. Come on. Dress up and we'll go out. I'll make it up to you."

Alex pressed her forehead against the wall to stop from shaking. Her voice broke. "I hate you. I really *hate* you!"

"I deserve that," Cliff said after a moment. "Give me another chance, Cone. I know I've got a vicious temper but you can help me. Only you! Cone, don't give up on me!"

He paused, waiting for her answer. When it didn't come he added, "Don't make me beg. Meet me, Cone. Please. I'll stand five feet away if you want. Please, honey. I can explain." His voice shook.

"No," she said, hardly able to quit shaking. "I can't help you. I don't know how. I don't want to even try anymore. And you already explained. You said it was my fault."

His voice rose in the intimidating way that always made her back down. "Who's been talking to you? Who's trying to poison you against me? Is it that creep Jenna? She never had a boyfriend in her life; what does she know? Relationships have ups and downs. Ask anyone!"

"Good-bye, Cliff."

"Don't hang up! Don't! Alex, listen! We need each other. I'll be by in fifteen minutes. If you're not home, I'll come to Jenna's."

Alex held the buzzing phone out for Jenna to hear. "He hung up!"

"Good! You told him off, right? That macho creep! He ought to go to jail."

She was so tired, but Cliff's command rang in her head. Already she was moving toward the door, drawn by an invisible magnet.

Jenna ran after her. "Don't go! How can you let him treat you like dirt? You're smart and pretty and creative. What's it gonna take for you to realize he's dangerous? *Alex*! Where are you going?"

"Home."

"Not to see *Cliff*?"

"No." She was suffocating. "I'm sorry, Jenna, I've got to get out of here. I need to be alone." Alex ran down the hall toward the front door.

Fifteen minutes later she was in bed with the covers pulled over her head. Her heart hurt so much that she didn't think she could stand it. She couldn't see him. She couldn't let him sweet-talk her into another chance. Not again. She wished her parents were home to make him go away. She shivered and cried. No more Cliff. How could she give up what she loved so much? How could she not?

When the bell rang, she covered her head and burrowed deeper under the covers.

Cliff rang again and again, each ring a blow to her senses. When the ringing didn't bring her he knocked, jiggled the knob, and pounded on the door. When she still didn't answer, he ran around to the side of the house and shouted, "Alex! Let me in! Give me a chance. Just one minute, that's all! Please!" She curled up into a tight ball, shut her eyes and jammed hands against her ears. Even so she heard every word until suddenly he stopped.

For the next ten minutes she lay rigid, waiting for him to come back from Jenna's. She thought of getting up and phoning her parents but couldn't bring herself to move. To tell Mom and Dad would be too awful. Dad might call the police. Everyone would find out!

Cliff returned. The bell rang again. And again. She heard the next-door neighbor shout that he should go away or he'd call the authorities. Cliff answered with curses and viciously kicked the door. "Alex! Damn it! I'm not going till you talk to me! Alex! Open up!" His voice faltered.

Like a sleepwalker, she slid out of bed, pulled on jeans and an old T-shirt and went down the stairs to the front door.

"Go away!" She called, pressing herself against the door.

"Alex honey! You're there! Let me in, just for a

minute. I swear I won't touch you. Just let me in for a minute!"

She squeezed her eyes tight shut and leaned her full weight against the door as if Cliff might break in if she didn't. No. She knew how it went. She'd forgive him and he'd be very loving for a while. He'd send flowers, give gifts, treat her like in the beginning. Then, out of the blue, it would start again. She'd do or not do something, say or not say something that didn't suit him. She could never predict what that would be. And then he'd do it again. Call her names, ignore her, embarrass her in front of others, push her around— rape her. Maybe beat her up so badly he'd break something. He was capable of it. He had a good role model—his father.

No. She couldn't give him another chance. It was her fault. She'd compromised too often. She deserved better.

"Cone!" Cliff called, shrill with annoyance. "For the last time! It's over, if you don't let me in! You hear me? Over!"

She put a hand on the knob, but quickly withdrew it. "Go away!" she screamed. "Go away, Cliff, or I'll call the police!"

"A-lex!" He pounded on the door so that it shuddered. He bellowed like a dangerous animal in pain.

Step by step she climbed the stairs back to her room, listening, terrified by the fury of his fists and voice. From far away she heard a siren. Had the neighbors phoned the police? *Oh, yes, please,* she hoped. But if they hadn't and Cliff didn't go away soon, now she knew that she would.